Lion and the Falcon

(Furry United Coalition, #4)

By
Eve Langlais

Copyright and Disclaimer

Edited by Brandi Buckwine
Copy Edited by Brienna Roberston
Produced in Canada

Published by Eve Langlais
1606 Main Street, PO Box 151
Stittsville, Ontario, Canada, K2S1A3
http://www.EveLanglais.com

ISBN-13: 978-1484849477
ISBN-10: 1484849477

Prologue

I'm free! I'm free! I'm free! He skipped along the sidewalk, big, hairy feet slapping out a beat as the two-word refrain repeated itself over and over in his head.

No more doctors. No more needles. No more restraints or peeing in a bottle. He had every reason in the world to sing. Dance. Do whatever he liked.

Because I'm free! Free! And completely lost.

Crap.

But he wouldn't let a little thing like not knowing exactly where he was burst his bubble. Loping through the barren streets, knuckles dragging on the ground, he breathed in lingering car exhaust fumes, a perfumed taste of freedom. Despite his currently location-challenged state, anything beat incarceration. Sure, *they* labeled it a safe house, but anything he couldn't freely leave he called a prison. One jailbreak later—featuring some screaming and bloodshed on the less than understanding part of the staff—and he got away not just from those determined to keep him under lock and key for his own safety, he also managed to escape the idiots he'd spent the last few years jailed with. If forced to listen one more time to how M87 lost his stupid eye, well, he might have gone crazy. Or at least crazier than he currently was.

Still, a little insanity after what he endured didn't give *them* the right to lock him away. How foolish to think once the mastermind's secret installation was discovered that he'd have true freedom. He'd simply traded one cell for another. Never mind the second prison boasted more comforts and didn't involve solitary confinement behind bars or torture. Who cared if the voices of those tending him spoke kindly and treated him well? He and the others rescued remained as always patients. And everyone knew what doctors and nurses did to patients.

Poking and prodding, asking questions, and drawing blood. Changing their title from experiments to guests didn't make the obtrusive testing and incarceration any better. The so-called FUC agents, and most especially the doctor, couldn't fix what was wrong with them. Couldn't erase what Mastermind did. Couldn't fill the hungry void inside. Couldn't cure the anger.

Nothing could erase the injustice meted to him and the others. The indignities—

Ooh, did he smell popcorn? Pausing in his escape, he sniffed the air. Again, the tantalizing aroma came to him; yummy, buttery popcorn coated in caramel. Saliva pooled in his mouth. *How long since I last tasted my favorite crunchy treat?*

Pivoting on a bare heel, he saw the letters of the façade first—Candy Shoppe. How original. Approaching the storefront, where a "Closed" sign hung, he faced the plate glass window and couldn't help but see the mirrored visage. The reflected monster startled him and he let out a yell as he stumbled away from the apparition. But putting himself out of reach didn't mean he didn't stare.

Yellow-eyed, jaw-slacked, and drooling over extended teeth, the abomination gazed right back. A niggle of unease shook him. He retreated a step and so did the creature. He waved. It waved as well. He growled, "Stay away from me!" only to see the hideous aberration's bulbous lips move at the same time. A sense of surreal horror gripped him.

No. It couldn't be. Forward he stepped. Once, twice, until his nose pressed against the cold, reflective glass and his mind grappled with the truth.

I am the monster.

He, once the most handsome man in his class—if one ignored his stunted height. The cutest monkey in his family when he shifted. The one slated for great things. Who once held a great job, wore suits, and enjoyed the delights of a different beauty every night—and not all of them paid by the hour—now, a creature of horror.

A whimper escaped him. *No! It's not fair.*

Mastermind had won. She'd finally succeeded after all this time. She'd turned his cute and cuddly side into a nightmarish creation. Oh the injustice of it. To survive intact all those years with her only to succumb when he should have been safe. He'd kill the rotten bitch, especially now that he could remember her face. Rip her tiny limbs from her body. Eat her black heart. Floss his teeth with her stringy hair. Do all kinds of despicable, monstrous things once he found her. It seemed only fair. And he was hungry. So very, very hungry…

First, though, he needed to take care of something else.

Glass smashed in an almost musical tinkle as he shoved his hairy fist through the offending partition. The scent of sweet and salty popcorn wafted out and he grabbed fistfuls of it, stuffing it in his mouth. Mmm. Popcorn.

He did so love popcorn. *Crunch. Crunch. Crunch.* Almost as much as he loved the idea of revenge.

Popcorn first. Then maybe some peanut brittle. Ooh, licorice.

Then, retribution.

Chapter One

Waking up Monday morning hung over from a weekend spent drinking too much and going to bed late sucked enough. Waking up to have his mother leaning over him frowning was enough to make any grown man scream like a little girl.

"What the hell, Mom!" Nolan yelled.

"Good morning to you too, son. Late night?"

Bare-chested, but thankfully wearing boxers, he nevertheless yanked the sheet up to his neck lest his mother check him for hickeys and give him heck for not sporting any. Lionesses enjoyed marking their conquests and his mother enjoyed seeing it, as she said it meant he at least attempted to do his part for the pride. But he'd come home alone last night and fallen into bed before he could stage a few with the vacuum.

In an effort to forestall her questions, he went on the offensive. "What are you doing here? How did you get in?" A valid question considering he'd just changed the locks—again—in the hopes of curbing her habit of popping in unexpectedly.

"I was worried about you. You haven't returned any of my texts or calls."

Intentionally. "I was busy."

"Too busy to call your poor mother?" Clutching at her chest, she batted her blonde lashes, but Nolan didn't fall for it. His mother, matriarch of the pride and pain in his furry ass, didn't have an innocent bone in her body. Although, he couldn't deny she cared. She just didn't care so much about his wellbeing as…

"How come you're sleeping alone?"

And here it came. "Because I prefer it that way."

"What happened to the ladies you were wining and dining last night?"

Ladies? Now that was a nicer term than he would have assigned to the she-cats sent, as he suspected, on his mother's orders. "You mean Jenny and Katie? Don't worry, Mom, they did their best to get me drunk and have their way with me. No need to punish them. Turns out, they can't handle their liquor as well as they thought." Especially when he cheated and poured a few of his shots in the glass of a grizzly named Buzz sitting beside him at the bar. Poor guy, he must have wondered why his glass never went empty—and why he woke up beside a bucktoothed cougar this morning.

Nolan would have to remember to send Buzz a bouquet of flowers and a bag of honeybuns as apology later today.

His mother's lips tightened into an almost invisible line. "So you didn't bed anyone last night? Or, according to my sources, the night before?"

He didn't know what he found more disturbing—the fact she was so well informed about his sex life, or the fact she lamented his lack of one. "Mom, this really isn't something I want to discuss." Ever. And especially not with her.

"I'm worried about you, Nolan. You're well past the age when you should have settled down with a harem."

Perish the thought. He had enough trouble with his existing female family members. Why would he want to add more? Besides, at just shy of thirty, he still had plenty of time to find Mrs. Right. "What you mean to say is why haven't I done my duty to the pride and fathered a few cubs for you to show off to the other clans. Has it occurred to you that perhaps I'd like to do things my way? You know, date a girl, fall in love, get married, then have kids? You know, the normal way?"

The appalled look on his mother's face almost made him laugh. Almost. But he knew better. The last person to do that still wore the scars. Son or not, his mother didn't take ridicule well. "Normal? There is nothing normal about you avoiding your duty to the family."

Nolan sighed. "I am not acting the part of stud, Mother."

"No one is asking you to."

"Then why do you keep trying to set me up with lionesses?" Or most recently, tigers. Apparently at this point, anything with a feline gene would do.

"I've got to do something. It's not like you're making any attempt to find the right women to impregnate and increase our pride."

Did she even listen to a word he said? Of course she didn't. When it came to the pride, and her role as leader within it, his mother possessed a one-track mind, a mind currently obsessed with getting her son laid. "Why can't you just relax and let me do things my way? In my own time? Did it ever occur to you that I'd like to find a woman who likes me for me and not because our families are trying to broker a deal? Or because you've promised them something?"

"I'm just looking out for you."

The hurt on her face appeared genuine. Guilt made him squirm. "I know you are." In her mind at least. In his, she meddled. Nolan didn't have an interest in acting as a baby-making machine, creating the next line of lions, or ligers, in order to appease his mother. It wasn't his fault he ended up the only male lion of age for their pride. Blame his sisters, cousins, and aunts who kept popping out girls and more girls. "Listen, Mom, can we talk about this later? I need to get up and get ready for work."

Not the best reminder, seeing how his mother hated his job, but at least it diverted her attention. She sniffed with clear disdain and lifted her nose in the air as she walked away from the bed, grabbing his clothes off the floor and tossing them in the hamper as she went. "I still can't believe you turned down that perfectly respectable job with the hospital"—which came with a big salary, an even nicer car than the one he currently drove, and all kinds of perks—"to work for *them.*" Them being FUC—the Furry United Coalition, helping shape-shifters worldwide since two thousand and eleven. Still a relatively new agency, the ones in power thought, given their population explosion, that it was time the shifters had their own police/protection agency. Previously, if a shifter required aid, they fended for themselves, which often caused more problems and attention than they wanted. No more. Now if a shifter needed help, they simply made a call and they got FUC'd. Not literally, of course, not that a few didn't try, their request for him specifically not always subtle.

"I like my job." More like loved, but he didn't need to irritate his mother any further, not when she proceeded to dust his dressers, her annoyance always resulting in cleaning. Needless to say, he didn't complain about that habit of hers and sometimes worked it to his advantage. It saved him from hiring a maid.

Despite his mother's lament that his current employment didn't come with a Jaguar and a giant office, or the prestige of a big hospital, Nolan did well for himself. He drove a nice car, lived in a great condo he'd bought with his own money, and in general had enough savings in the bank to tempt any woman. Until they met his mother. Then any normal female, who had any kind of mental capacity, would run the other way, probably screaming. He'd seen it before. It would take a strong personality to counter that of his overbearing mother. Problem was Nolan preferred women with docile characteristics, the complete opposite, in other words.

Once upon a time, he thought he had found the right girl. Stephanie. A hot cougar with a few years on him. She was a business woman with a decent job, money of her own and an independent spirit. Best of all, she dated him because she actually liked him, and not just because of his looks or position. It only took his mother's sudden appearance at the head of his bed, dispensing advice while Steph rode cowgirl, for her to disappear, her text message of, *"It's not you, it's your mother,"* not really much of a surprise.

"I can't see how you can like being underpaid, underappreciated, and overworked." Again with the sniff.

Put in that light, it sounded foolish, however, he knew better. Nolan enjoyed the people he worked with, what they stood for, and the fact his mother couldn't dictate to them. Helping those in trouble and meting out justice also appealed to his chivalrous side. Not that expressed that aloud. In his mother's world, altruism was for the weak. Only cold, hard cash and power counted. He'd argued enough times with her since his decision to join the agency to know it was pointless to try and change her mind.

"Mom…" he injected a warning tone in the drawn out word.

A moue of distaste twisted her features, more to do he suspected with the wine stain on his beige slacks—which he'd forgotten to soak before climbing in to bed last night—than because of the topic at hand. She tossed the offending item into his hamper. "Fine. Break a poor mother's heart. If your father were alive, he'd die of shame."

If his father were alive, he would probably be deaf, or living somewhere without phones or mail service deep in the jungle. "Goodbye, Mother."

"I'm leaving. For now. I can tell when I'm not wanted."

Really? Mark it on the calendar as a first.

"But keep in mind, we aren't finished discussing this. You will do your duty to the pride."

Or else. Yeah, yeah. He'd heard the speech. Had it painted over, too, in the bathroom, living room, and even his bedroom ceiling, his mother's attempt to get him to see her point of view posted in black and white. At least she had not managed to tattoo it on his body—yet. He'd foiled the last two attempts by recognizing the sleeping agent slipped into his drinks. Threatening to move to San Francisco to join the gay male pride living there put a stop to that.

Lying in bed, he waited until he heard the click of the door before hopping out from under the covers. Stretching, he scratched his lightly furred belly before stripping off his boxers and dropping them to the floor. He didn't worry too much about leaving a mess. Never did. As the only male of breeding age in the pride, he was more than spoiled. But given what he put up with, he felt the few perks he got, such as free laundry and cleaning, were well deserved.

He hit the shower, his golden mane requiring daily washing, conditioning, and blow drying to keep it fluffy and soft. As he went through his ritual, he wondered what the day would bring.

The last few weeks had proven busy. Since the mastermind's demise, he and the medical staff in the FUC safe-house-turned-infirmary spent a lot of time trying to recapture the escaped patients and dealing with the aftermath, mainly, the fact that with her final act and injection of a virulent toxin, Mastermind irrevocably changed the patients in his care, and not in a good way. Already, Nolan lost three of the patients they recaptured, the changes in their body too much for their cells to handle. And another two weren't far behind.

Whatever Mastermind gave to those poor shape-shifters, it was nasty. It turned the most mundane of people, the gentlest of creatures, into horrible monsters. When it worked. Sometimes, the morph only partially happened, leaving the poor victim in a halfway state. Painful and debilitating, the only solution when that happened was to inject them with heavy doses of morphine to control the pain.

Not good. And if that was what he dealt with at the safe house, then what about the ones still at large? How did they cope? Because it wasn't just the whole shifting and intense pain thing that proved an issue. When the cocktail didn't kill or bring its victim to their knees, screaming, whatever the injection contained brought out violent tendencies. Turned even the most docile of people into maniacal killers.

No one would ever forget the first time the victims swapped into their new, horrible selves. It happened the night Mastermind escaped. Caught up in the drama Mastermind left when they discovered her identity, they paid little attention to the experiments, the patients who still seemed normal on the outside. But inside their bodies, science and mutations were hard at work.

In the wee hours of night, the patients morphed, slaughtering the poor guards and night staff in the safe house. Nolan was on the phone with one of the guards when it happened. He would never forget the screams. Even more chilling were the words of a patient blaming Nolan for their current state.

"We'll be seeing each other soon, doc-tor. Bloody soon." The chilling laughter at the end of that

statement still woke him up in a cold sweat and had him looking over his shoulder all too often. It also hurt his feelings.

How could the patients think he played a part in Mastermind's heinous plot when all he had done was try to cure them? Did his best to help them recover from the experimentation Mastermind conducted? But angry, drugged, and no longer in their right minds, the poor victims needed someone to blame. Who better than the handsome—and modesty lacking, but always truthful—doctor in charge of them?

Worry over their possible revenge cut into his naptime. Working on just ten to fourteen hours of somnolence a day really made him cranky. Everyone knew lions needed their sleep. Despite his fatigue, he worked harder than ever as he tried to forget the sibilant whisper the night everything went to hell. As a brave and majestic beast, usually the threat of one individual would never throw him for such a loop—if it weren't for the fact that those they recaptured expressed the same sentiment, and not just toward him, but his entire staff.

"I'm going to hunt you and skin you, then eat you alive," threatened one.

"Juicy, juicy nurse. Won't you give me a bite?" begged another.

"Meat! Meat! The magic fruit, the more you eat the more you want more," screamed another, in an attempt at poetry fallen short.

At least he could defend himself, unlike some of the others. King of the jungle and all that. *Hear me roar!*

To think the mastermind had hidden under their very noses. *I should have known.* Suspected, at the very least, given how the diminutive figure always seemed to lurk around every corner, listening and watching. But really, who would have thought the teeny tiny squirrel mix with the thick glasses was the maniac behind the kidnappings, killings, and experimentation on shifters? Nolan never once gave the ugly little woman a second glance. None of them did.

They'd paid the price for their neglect, some more than others. When his mother found out how close he'd tread to danger, he'd worried she'd make good on her threat to lock him up to keep him safe. He remembered all too well the summer of the bubble.

Fall out of a tree just once and break an arm… You'd have thought the world ended. After that incident, she wouldn't let him out to play without first putting him a plastic bubble that rolled around, making him appear like a hamster in a ball. It took him falling in a river, floating downstream, and taking a ride over the falls for his mother to realize her plan to protect him might have some drawbacks. Padding, banning him from outdoor play, and other ridiculous measures were enacted until he bore the saddest kitty face imaginable.

Thankfully, sanity—the rest of the pride's, not his matriarch's—prevailed. His aunts came to his rescue and advised his mother that he was the laughing stock of the rival prides. Well, if there was one thing his mother couldn't abide, aside from seeing him hurt, it was not basking in the respect she deserved.

She'd switched tactics after that by instead enrolling him in a defense and gymnastics class, figuring the less clumsy he was, the less likely to injure himself. Not the lacrosse or baseball he dreamed of playing, but at least it beat the alternatives. And he learned how to bloody the noses of those who made fun of him.

A grown man now, Mother dear had loosened the apron strings somewhat, just not by choice. Nolan forced the issue every chance he got, insisting on moving out, choosing his own career and work locale. He even forewent a personal groomer—but not his hairdresser. Some things, like his mane, required special attention. A lion with a messy head of hair was just unacceptable. He couldn't explain why. It just was.

Which was why, despite running late, he still took the time to indulge in a long, hot shower. He washed his hair, conditioned it, and blow dried it in layers then dressed in impeccably pressed slacks and a shirt before he made his way to work, running a tad behind schedule. It didn't help he forgot he needed to hit their main office instead of the safe house first—Kloe, the leader of FUC for this area, having called a general meeting.

Arriving at headquarters, he ran the usual gauntlet. Lisa at front reception who leaned over as often as possible to show off her ample cleavage; Beatrice from accounting who not so subtly hinted she'd meet him anytime, anywhere; and Zoe, who, despite being married to her fourth husband and older than his mother, still made every attempt to get in his pants. Now there was a lady he made sure to avoid at staff parties.

Nolan bore their attention with good grace, even if it made him uncomfortable. None of these women liked him because they knew him. They approved what he did for a living—who didn't want a doctor as a boyfriend or potential son-in-law? They admired his looks—blond, clean cut, and always dressed in a suit. They enjoyed his politeness—opening doors, holding out chairs, using his "please" and "thank yous" as if his mother would tolerate any rudeness from her son. They tittered at his sense of humor—a necessary trait to diffuse many a situation, considering the number of women he grew up with. His lack of modesty meant he recognized his status as a good catch. But, despite all his awesome outward attributes, he could honestly say none of the women who flirted with him, who made every attempt to get in his pants, knew the real him.

It might have made him abnormal in some guy's eyes that he rejected, nicely of course, their advances, but he really had no other choice. It bothered him that none of the women he ever met ever seemed interested in anything deeper. *Doesn't anyone want to get to know the real me? To see the man below the handsome veneer?*

Despite their shallow interest, he still bestowed a bright smile on the cheerful female manning the reception desk for the FUC office. "Hello, Lisa."

"Good morning, Dr. Manners."

"Please, I've told you before to call me Nolan. Doctor makes me sound so old."

She blushed and fluttered her lashes. "Oh, I couldn't."

"But I insist."

"Okay…Nolan." She giggled.

"And how are you doing today?"

Again, she turned pink. "Great. Thanks so much for asking."

Okay, so he purposely turned on the charm. He didn't want to appear rude. "Anything pressing I should know about?"

"Just the usual." Which could mean anything from nothing going on to alligators in the sewer. Lisa's answer never wavered, the sign of a good receptionist.

The phone on her desk buzzed. "Uh—oh, that's the board room. I better answer it." She lifted the receiver and said, "Hello." Then, "Right away," before hanging up with a sheepish grin, which she pointed in his direction. "That was

Kloe. Somehow, it slipped my mind to mention they're all waiting for you in the meeting room."

Checking his watch, Nolan groaned. Darn it. He was really late. Again. "I'd better get going."

Off he went up the hall, making sure to flash a grin at Beatrice who practically swooned in delight. He strode into the meeting-in-progress, hoping against hope no one would notice his tardy arrival. Yeah, right.

All conversation ceased as more than a half dozen eyes veered his way, but it was the sneeringly said, "I see Sylvester finally arrived," that ruffled the hair of his mane.

Tossing his golden strands back, he did his best to appear apologetic. "Sorry I'm late. I was unavoidably detained. I hope I didn't miss too much."

"Detained, or distracted by a mirror," he heard in a low mutter from someone he didn't recognize.

With a shake of her matronly head, Kloe spoke. "So nice of you to join us, Nolan. I was beginning to wonder if some of our patients took a turn for the worse."

"Not since I was in touch with them in the last half hour." He'd called the safe house staff on his way over. Difficulties arriving on time didn't mean he shirked his responsibilities.

Miranda, very much pregnant and still as energetic as ever, bounced in her seat. "Hi, Nolan. We were just getting started. Come sit beside me. I saved you a seat."

She patted the chair beside her and he wanted to groan. There was a reason only Chase, her husband, sat close by. Before pregnancy, Miranda had enough energy to power a small town. Pregnant? Good grief, the woman turned into a nonstop chatterbox with absolutely no boundaries and an insatiable, sometimes deadly, urge for carrot cake.

However, latecomers couldn't be picky, and the seat beside her was the only one available, limiting his options. Sliding into the chair, he tried to ignore the rapier stare of the woman across from him, a woman he'd never met, but who obviously knew something of him given her rude remarks. What he couldn't figure out was her instant dislike of him. Then again, given she smelled like some species of bird and he was a lion, he could probably chalk the animosity to an instinctual thing.

It still rankled, though, especially when she tossed a scornful look his way. He fought an urge to stick out his tongue and focused on Kloe's words.

"Now that we're all here, let's get down to business. We received more reports last night via our contact in the police department of monster sightings. So far, the cops are treating the calls as pranks. Lucky for us, they're assuming what people saw were wild animals or folks in costume, but we can't keep letting this happen. It's only a matter of time before someone catches one of the escaped victims, who are proving to be less than discreet. We can't let the normals discover our secret."

Humans plus the knowledge that shape-shifters existed among them equaled a very bad idea. No one disagreed with that. Look at what happened to the poor alien who landed years ago, a messenger for his race looking to see if Earth wanted to sign a trade treaty. The American government still refused to apologize to the Hlin'unger nation for the testing they'd put the poor guy through. It wasn't just the Martians who apparently held a fetish for anal probes. Thankfully, the galaxy travelers weren't the violent sort or Earth would have ended up a pile of galactic dust by now. Needless to say, Earth didn't get invited into the Galactic version of the United Nations.

"Computer mapping of the sightings shows they've spread out and have infested all corners of the city and even some of the suburbs. They're not going to be easy to find. We need more agents," Jessie, their office geek, announced without looking up from her laptop.

"Haven't the reinforcements arrived yet?" Mason asked, twirling a honey donut around his finger, probably to annoy his brother who stared at the pastry with hunger even though he had a plateful in front of him. Darned bears, they hated sharing sweets.

Kloe cleared her throat and shifted in her seat. "About the reinforcements. Apparently, the escaped projects aren't the only problem plaguing our citizens right now. Out west, they're dealing with a sudden explosion in giant rats, which they're still struggling to identify as the regular or shape-shifting variety. Up north, our Canadian friends are caught up in a Sasquatch crisis. The sea folk are dealing with an oil spill. And as for our avian counterparts, while I am unsure of the reason, they haven't been able to spare us the air troops we'd hoped for."

"So what did we get?" Viktor asked with his usual bluntness.

"Me."

The one word, spoken with quiet confidence, of course came from the lady sitting across from Nolan. He took a moment to study her as she stood to address the group.

Tall, real tall, and thin, she didn't have the curves Nolan preferred. The avian agent sported a muscled leanness from her wiry arms—shown off in a short sleeve black shirt—to her boyishly slim hips from which her black cargo pants hung. Her long black hair, held back in a tight ponytail, highlighted an equally angular face with sharp lips, a straight nose, and no-nonsense, aqua eyes. Not classically pretty, she possessed presence and exuded arrogance. A real ball buster, he'd wager, and totally not his type. He preferred his woman petite, soft, and unable to hurt him. He got enough grief from his mother and other female relatives, enough that he saw no reason to put up with it in his personal life as well.

"My name is Clarice Tertius, ASS agent with a specialty in hunting. I was assigned by my department to assist you in your search. I can provide avian support as well as ground having trained in tracking."

A throat cleared. "No offense, but how is one bird supposed to help us locate a dozen missing psychos?"

"They're not psychos," Nolan objected.

Viktor's hard gaze pinned him. "The last one we caught was chewing on its own tail. If that's not crazy then I'd hate to see what you think crazy is."

Nolan spread his hands as if apologizing for them. "It's not their fault. The toxin the mastermind injected them with is affecting their cognitive abilities."

"So in other words, lizard guy over there is right," interrupted Clarice. "They're nuts."

"Sick."

"Either way, Sylvester, they need to be found and brought in. Not only for their own good, but the good of everyone."

"I think at this point, given their violent tendencies, we should be shooting them on sight," Viktor advanced. Not surprising, given the croc's solution to every problem involved guns.

Lucky for him, even Renee couldn't let her mate's suggestion go by without objection. "We can't do that. It's not their fault. Nolan is right about that."

"But we also can't let them keep running around destroying the city and scaring the locals," Miranda added without her usual giggle. "Sorry, Nolan, but Viktor and Clarice are correct in that respect. If we can't capture them, then we need to stop them, even if it means deadly force. I'd volunteer to help, but until junior here GETS OUT!"—she yelled the last bit to her protruding belly—"then you're stuck with second best." Someone was getting testy as her pregnancy entered the final stage.

Viktor cleared his throat.

"Sorry, old partner. I meant third best."

Mason coughed.

Miranda twitched her nose in his direction and he slouched in his chair. "Something wrong, dear brother in law?"

"Nope, just something caught in my throat."

"Thought so. As I was saying, I'd like to help, but since I can't, you'll have to make do with the chickadee."

"Excuse me? Did you just dis me, rabbit?" The avian agent turned her rapier glare on Miranda.

"Just telling it like it is, *birdy*." Miranda's sweet tone didn't fool anyone for a minute; however, the newcomer apparently didn't know better. Nolan wondered if he should duck for cover.

"Are you trying to tell me that you think you're better than me?" Her thin brows arched up and a sneer stretched Clarice's lips. "Let me guess, your floppy ears are trained in kung fu. Do you slap your prey silly with the fuzzy tips until they fall over begging for mercy? Or tickle them with your fur?"

Miranda's eyes narrowed dangerously. "Ooh, if I could unleash my furry beast, you wouldn't be laughing, Tweety."

"Watch what you call me, fluffy bunny."

"I'll show you fluffy!" Miranda's mood swung from irritable to violent in a second and it took Chase throwing an arm in front of her to keep her from leaping from her seat.

With his face sporting a weary expression, Chase rumbled, "I wouldn't antagonize her if I were you, Ms. Tertius. Her favorite bakery didn't have her usual morning carrot muffins so she's a little on edge. And, despite her advanced condition, she's still quite dangerous."

"Oh, are you talking about the bakery up the street? That would be my fault. I bought those muffins to feed to the pigeons in the park." Clarice smiled and a minor moment of chaos erupted as even Chase couldn't halt his wife from sprinting over the table with more agility than a pregnant woman should be capable of. Luckily, Mason, used to his sister-in-law's antics, caught Miranda and only let out one girlish squeal as she kneed him in the groin. Chase, with his face set in a forbearing expression, scooped up his screaming wife and set her on her feet behind his massive frame, blocking her from going after the taunting ASS agent. It didn't stop the threats, though.

"I'm going to clip your wings, Tweety! Pluck your feathers. Pull—" Her imaginative yells of retribution cut off short as her phone beeped and she paused to look at the screen. Miranda squealed, "Ooh, the bakery just texted me. My muffins are ready."

Off she bounced, and Chase sighed. "We'll be back after she's stuffed her face."

"Don't hurry, teddy," Clarice taunted.

Everyone winced as the big grizzly turned to face their temporary avian aide. "If I were you, I'd stay far, far away once the baby is born. You don't want to mess with my floppy-eared menace. She's got big teeth."

Nolan could tell Clarice didn't understand, but those who knew Miranda? Yeah, they'd probably place bets on the outcome.

Silence and order more or less returned. Kloe, who tended to not get involved with Miranda these days, preferring to let Chase handle his wife, pushed her reading glasses up on her nose and cleared her throat. "Yes, so where were we?"

"Discussing the fact we might need to use deadly force if we can't take the missing subjects quietly." Victor, never one to let outbursts ruffle his cool demeanor, picked up where they left off.

"I object. They're people. Just give me a chance. I'm sure there must be a way to help them," Nolan spoke up in their defense.

"Your objection is noted, but sorry, doctor, I fear the agents are right. We can't allow them to keep terrorizing the city. All in favor of deadly force?"

Okay, so his jutting lower lip might have appeared childish as the voices overruled his, but they didn't understand. He'd taken an oath, an oath to heal and protect. Sure, he might lead the life of careless bachelor and spoiled son of the biggest pride around, but at heart, Nolan was a healer. Helping others was what he did. Guilt riddled him that he'd not done more for the victims when they were under his care. As it was, feeling as if he failed them, he fought an urge to not have a tantrum like Miranda.

The day went from annoying to worse. Once the meeting ended, he skipped his morning nap and headed over to the safe house, a nondescript brownstone converted into a makeshift hospital. Despite his speed in arriving, he walked in to discover that of the two victims they had recovered, one died while he was en route and the other slipped into a coma.

Great. Just bloody great. Shutting himself in his office, he did what any self-respecting lion would do in his situation. He ate a package of Hot Rods and took a nap.

Chapter Two

What a bunch of incompetent idiots. And I have to work with them until further notice.

Clarice simmered as she took the stairs two at a time down to street level. Unbelievable. Tell one stupid vain bird high up in the avian food chain to take a flight, and next thing she knew, she got reassigned to FUC duty. An ASS agent expected to give herself over to FUC.

How demeaning.

Never mind her boss couched her dishonorable department transfer in terms like "Best hunter we have," "Improving interspecies relationships," and "Time to cool off." She saw her deployment for what it was. A slap in the face for saying *no* to the son of the guy in charge of Avian Soaring Security. Okay, so her no might have involved a bloody nose, a sprained wrist, and threats to his manhood. Still, what did he expect when he grabbed her ass? Not that anyone cared she was the recipient of sexual harassment. They expected her to look the other way and forgive the strutting peacock. Not likely. Nor would she forgive them for punishing her. When she finished this assignment, she was so going to stuff some chestnuts where the sun didn't shine and roast some ASS over coals. And despite the wagers to the contrary, she would succeed in solving the FUC problem just to spite her old boss and his fowl—probably descended from a turkey—excuse of a son.

Now that she'd met the FUC team, she could see why they needed her expertise. A crocodile with no sense of smell. A bear who worked as a lawyer when he wasn't stuffing his face with honey buns. Another bear who didn't take anything seriously. A crazy, pregnant rabbit—who would give Bugs Bunny a run for his money. And a blonde kitty cat doctor who wanted to save criminals instead of putting them down. No wonder they were stuck and in need of help.

It amazed her they had ever managed to track down the mastermind and her lair in the first place. Then again, they didn't so much capture the mastermind as inadvertently sweep her up with all her victims, taken in by her diminutive size, thinking she was one of the prisoners instead of the one in charge.

Sloppy work.

Well, it wouldn't happen anymore. Not on her watch.

While Jessie, the Swan king's very own daughter and resident tech geek, worked on fine-tuning the mapping of the sightings and possible hiding spots, Clarice decided to visit the safe house and talk to the staff. Get a feel for the *things* she hunted. She wanted the fine details, the items nurses and orderlies didn't put in files. Those small clues might make the difference when it came to finding the psychos at large. She just hoped she could avoid the annoying Dr. Manners.

She couldn't have pinpointed exactly what about the guy irritated her, although his good looks were part of it. A blond Adonis who, despite being dressed in a suit, appeared more like a tanned surfer than a doctor in charge of saving lives. Think of the most good-looking doctor on television, multiply it by ten, and you'd probably come up with Nolan Manners. Add to it his superiority complex and feline heritage and she was predisposed to hate him just on principle. She was a bird. Blame it on her genes.

Winging her sport bike through traffic and getting stuck at a train crossing meant it took her longer than she expected to make it to the safe house. Yet, despite that, she managed to park in the spot marked "Reserved for the doctor." Did she care it probably belonged to Dr. Manners? Not really. Lazy cat should have gotten his furry ass to work on time. Besides, no way would she leave her two-wheeled baby on the road where uncaring motorists could scratch it. Let the doctor park his BMW or Mercedes, or whatever the pretentious prick drove, on the street. It would serve him right for taking his time. Late to the meeting. Taking his sweet time getting to work. Her impression of him just got better and better.

Swaggering to the front door, leathers creaking, helmet in hand, her aviator glasses hid her eyes from the worst of the sun's glare. She stabbed the buzzer, but instead of a voice on the intercom asking her to state her business, the door swung open and she got a surprise.

"What took you so long?" Dr. Manners asked, his smile a touch too wide and toothy.

"How did you get here before me?" she sputtered, taken aback at his appearance.

"I drove," he replied with a smirk. "I'll admit, I expected you much sooner. It took you so long to arrive, I even had time to take a nap."

A nap? She eyed his perfect hair and unwrinkled appearance and figured he pulled her drumstick.

"Are you coming in, or are we going to give the neighborhood something to talk about?"

In she stepped, dancing out of the way as he swung the heavy portal shut with a metal clang that belied the scarred, wooden exterior façade. Though the brownstone appeared benign from the outside, hidden beneath its veneer was a bunker style residence. Not that it did them any good when they'd harbored the most feared criminal within its very walls.

The familiar scent of hospital antiseptic washed over her. How she hated that smell and the reminder of how she ended up an orphan of the state. Squashing memories, she flipped her glasses up on her head and peered around. "Pretty slick setup, Sylvester."

"My name is Nolan."

"Whatever. I'm bad with remembering names." The smile she flashed was not exactly nice, but the best she could manage. He brought out the nasty in her. "What do the neighbors think you have going on in here?"

"Botox clinic."

"For real?"

He shrugged. "It's worked quite well as a cover so far. Especially when we get shifters caught in a half morph or who are injured. People ignore the bandages and head wraps because of the cover story. But I'm sure you didn't come here to quiz me about our setup. I assume you want to question the staff who worked with some of the patients and review video footage, what little we have of the night in question."

What she really wanted to do was get ahead of the doctor and call the shots, something he'd not allowed since she got her foot in the door. Having pegged him as an idiot who got the job because of his looks and pedigree, she did not like how he seemed determined to smash her preconceptions by predicting what she thought.

"If you'll just show me to a room I can use and give me a list of the staff, I can conduct the interviews while you get on with your own work."

A sad expression crossed his face as he shrugged. "What work? The only patient I have left slipped into a coma and I don't expect they'll survive the night. At this point, I've done everything I can. Now, I need to wait on test results to see if anything I've tried has made a difference."

"Tried, as in…?" Not that she possessed much medical knowledge, but even she had to wonder what the doctor thought he could achieve. Mutant movies all seemed to have one resounding theme in common. Once a person's genes got messed with, forget turning them back to normal.

"From the information we've gleaned, the mastermind was obsessed with enhancing certain shifter aspects. She wanted the ability to make a shifter bigger, more aggressive, and stronger."

"Why?"

"Why does any power hungry being do anything? To intimidate others. To feel in control. Given what little we've discovered, I've formulated a theory that given her diminutive size, the mastermind suffered from megalomania and a Napoleon complex."

Her brow knitted at the expressions. She'd never done well at biology, or psychology, or anything that ended in ology.

Apparently, he grasped this because he explained in normal terms she could follow, the jerk. "She was obsessed with doing great things and being recognized for them while at the same time battling with the feeling of being too small. The mastermind overcompensated by being overly aggressive and controlling. In other words, she believed herself smarter than us all, but it wasn't enough. She also wanted to be big enough to fight her own battles and have people fear her."

"So she was looking for a way to change herself into a monster?"

"Well, I'm pretty sure she didn't mean for that aspect to happen. Jessie's still working on pulling up background information on Mastermind. Most of it was obliterated, probably intentionally. The interviews we've conducted, though, from classmates who recalled Mastermind growing up, those who survived, that is, gave a picture of someone who hated her shifter side. When it came to the gene pool, she truly got the short end of the stick. And I mean short. She had poor eyesight, little muscle tone, was undersized, and in general the weakest of the weak. A victim of bullying, Mastermind wanted to change that."

"By becoming the bully." Clarice wanted to sneer at the doctor's empathy and understanding, but he'd obviously placed a lot of time and thought into the motive behind Mastermind's actions. He also seemed to genuinely want to help those the psycho bitch hurt. It messed with her perception of him as a jerk.

"Essentially, yes. She didn't seem to realize that her increased intelligence more than made up for a lack of physical ability. So she experimented from an early age, but never on herself. At least, until the end. It seemed the work I did on reversing the effects of her testing had her stumble along the solution she had looked for all along. I inadvertently gave her the ability to turn on a regressive DNA strand harkening back to our primitive origins."

"Whoa, wait a second. She turned those patients into what, cave men?"

"Not quite. She found a way to switch on the prehistoric versions of their animals with some added modifications. What she didn't factor in was that thousands of years ago, brain sizes and capabilities were much smaller."

"So in making her animal side stronger, she in essence made herself stupider."

"The loss of cognitive ability and intelligence were an unfortunate result of too much testosterone, possible hypoglycemia, and the increased body mass reducing blood flow to the more logical parts of the brain."

She more or less followed his scientific explanation and summarized it. "So when she shifted, all her blood left her brain, kind of like a man when he gets a hard-on. Gotcha."

Finally, she flustered the doctor. Clearing his throat, he grabbed his tie and tugged on it. "Um, yes, I guess you could compare it to that."

"So she got what she wanted and injected herself. I got that from reading the report about her takedown, but why did she inject everyone else at the safe house? Wouldn't it have been more logical for her to keep them as weak victims, people she could dominate?"

"Keep in mind that at this point Mastermind was no longer entirely rational. From what we could piece together, she expected the patients to thank her for what she did and become her willing minions. Things didn't quite work out that way."

"According to one of the inmates—"

"Victims."

"—they laughed at her and she ran off."

"Yes. But we didn't find out about her injections until much later."

"Because she'd managed to hack your computer systems and put the safe house in lockdown mode." She smirked. "Outsmarted by a nutsy squirrel. That had to burn, eh, Sylvester? So what did you do?"

"Me? Nothing. We were stuck in lockdown in a dark room with no food." Again, he rolled his wide shoulders and she couldn't help but notice the size of him, and not from fat. "I napped. It was Jessie who managed to hack back into the computers and eventually send out an SOS to the main FUC office to get us out."

"But the patients hadn't yet escaped or changed at this point."

"No. That happened later that night." With devastating results. Again, sadness shadowed his expression. She almost felt bad for the guy. He'd not just lost coworkers that night, but probably some friends.

"So all of the patients were infected?"

"Every single last one. Two, though, never made it out the door. Their bodies just couldn't handle it. The others busted out of here and split off."

"Without any tracking devices." Clarice shook her head in disbelief.

Nolan's expression turned defensive. "You can't be serious? Why would we chip them? These were people, not criminals or pets," he snapped.

"They were unknowns in FUC custody with abilities that made them dangerous before the mastermind screwed with them further. You should have tagged them."

"Well, we didn't."

"A pity. It would have made my job easier. Back to the psychos on the loose. What kind of mutations are we talking about? Extra teeth? Hulklike shifting? Super strength?"

"Despite the energy it requires, yes, size is one of the most common things we've noted they have in common. Expect them in shifted mode to have a body mass two to five times denser than normal, if not more."

The estimate made her brows arch. "How is that possible?"

He shrugged. "How can any of us shift in the first place? There's obviously more at work than just simple genetics. The kind of weight we'd be talking about otherwise condensed when they're in human form would make it impossible for any organs to function. Much as I hate to use the word magic or inexplicable, something makes it possible. You should see Renee when she turns into her fox. She's the size of a minivan."

"No way."

"Oh yes, and if you even think of looking at her croc, she's liable to eat you. Good thing she's on our side."

"Wait a second. Isn't she one of the people you rescued? How come she's allowed to roam free?"

"Renee was a patient of Mastermind's, but as a study subject. Her special ability stems from a childhood incident involving a radioactive vat. Something about her mutation makes her resistant to drugs so Mastermind's experiments didn't work on her. But you needn't worry about Renee. She's quite docile, unless like I mentioned, you threaten those she loves."

Clarice rubbed at her forehead. "Why does this mission keep getting more and more complicated?"

"It's only because you're new to FUC. Once you get used to our methods and the staff, you'll find it much easier to follow. Heck, you might even fall in love with FUC and never want to leave."

"I prefer ASS."

"Excuse me?"

"You might like FUC, but I'm an ASS girl, as in Avian Soaring Security. No mutant birds or mad scientists in our outfit."

"Wrong. Apparently, you didn't read the whole file. We've got a bird on the loose. From the reports, we think it's an ostrich mixed with pterodactyl."

Clarice blinked, but he remained dead serious. "Okay. I see I'm going to need to do some serious reading tonight. In the meantime, let's go back to physical changes that seem universal among the changed patients. Let's start with their muscles."

"Overly developed. It's like each and every one gets pumped up, whether needed or not. Instant twelve packs, and quads, and pecs. It's quite disconcerting."

Having seen enough body builders on steroids to know, she couldn't help but agree. "Teeth and claws are elongated?"

"Think saber-toothed and add a few inches in some cases. I know Mastermind thought she'd found the switch to spring us forward evolution wise, but if you ask me, the switch she turned on in the DNA strands was a step back into the past. I mean, the dentition we've estimated on some of the mutations is ridiculous."

"Dinosaur-sized in other words."

"Yes."

"So where does the violence stem from? You said something about increased testosterone and decreased mental capacity. But that doesn't explain the rage. I've heard the recordings of that night. They all seem so…angry." Beyond angry, bloodthirsty. Or as one of the psychos said, "hungry."

"I'm not sure if it's a side effect of the change or just an enhancement of their issues stemming from captivity. Don't forget, these people were victims kept in horrifying conditions. Many of them hadn't seen the light of day in years. Some, like Renee, were captive so long she didn't even recall what the sky or sun looked like. Add in a heavy dose of hormones, a primitive urge for survival, and they did what any animal who feels hunted or in danger would do. They lashed out."

"Now you're stretching. These aren't teenagers rebelling. These are full-grown people. Adults. They know right from wrong."

"But they had their brains tampered with. Are they really responsible for their actions?"

"They ate your staff."

He winced. "Only some of them."

"Raw." Her nose wrinkled as she said it.

"Yeah." He slumped.

"So, they suffer from 'roid rage times a hundred. What else?"

"According to my testing, their healing ability is compromised mostly because of the energy they expend while in shift mode. They require large quantities of vitamins and nutrients to replenish themselves and have to rest after every change."

"So lots of food and sleep. Gotcha. If we can mobilize quick enough after an attack then we might be able to catch them while they're recuperating."

"I thought the plan was to catch them before they hurt anyone."

"In a perfect Pollyana world, we would. However, do I need to remind you of how well that hasn't been working for you? If we knew where they were, you wouldn't need me. Correction, you would still need me, but I wouldn't be wasting my time talking to you instead of being out there hunting them down."

"Rescuing."

"Whatever, Sylvester."

"Nolan."

"I told you I was bad with names. So how many animals we talking about on the loose? And what kind?"

"Again, it's in the files."

Ugh, again with the reading. "Humor me."

"A dozen are still roaming, if they survived. Amphibian, ostrich, chimp, two from the squirrel family, a doe—"

"A deer?"

"A female deer."

Okay, she wasn't going to start humming that stupid song she learned in school. No. No. Too late. The next verse started in her head as he went on reciting the animals.

"A domestic cat, a gecko, and four unknowns."

"Unknown?"

"They couldn't recall their shifter animal and their records were missing. One has the appearance of a melted candle mixed with slime, but the other three, even though we put them through DNA testing, came out undetermined."

"So we've got a full menu of shifters, each with different abilities running free. Lovely. Well, thanks for answering my questions."

"That's it?"

"For now. I might have more questions later. If you could show me to that room you promised me for interviews and send in the staff who treated them, then I get can started."

"Of course." The doctor spun in his polished loafers and headed up the hall, the lack of a white coat leaving his butt on display. A fine display. Not that Clarice admired it. Okay, maybe she did. Blame her acute vision, which forced her to notice just how nicely he filled out his pants. Ugh. *There is something so wrong about a bird wondering what a cat's butt would look like naked.*

Dr. Manners left her alone in a windowless, nondescript room after ascertaining she didn't want his help. Clarice conducted her interviews with the staff who worked with the maniacs on the loose. None of them had much to add other than several of the patients really hated medical personnel, they feared for their safety, and Dr. Manners was just dreamy. It made Clarice wonder if it wasn't just the patients they drugged around here.

Unlike the doctor, though, the staff all seemed agreed on one point. The psychos on the loose should be stopped at all cost. Lucky for them, they had the best ASS agent on the job.

Chapter Three

Talking with Clarice left Nolan unsettled. Something about her roused his feline, and not in a hunt-the-bird-down-and-swallow-her-whole kind of way, but more like an I-want-to-lick-her-up-and-down fashion to see if he could ruffle her unflappable feathers. He blamed his inappropriate urge on fatigue because he refused to entertain the notion she attracted him. Dominant women were not his type, even if he could so easily picture Clarice in a skin tight, leather cat suit—made of synthetic fiber, of course—wielding her sharp tongue in ways meant to pleasure a man. Drool.

No and no. He shoved the erotic image away. Hot or not, he didn't date—willingly at any rate—strong-minded females. They reminded him too much of his mother and the rest of the females in his family. Shudder.

After he checked on his comatose patient—no change—he ducked off to his office for a short nap. When he woke, Clarice had left, and his patient remained unresponsive. More discouraging, the test results had returned. Nothing he had attempted treatment wise showed any positive effect. The DNA changes remained locked.

Brainstorming in front of a whiteboard, already scribbled with ideas, didn't give him any fresh insights. *I don't know what to do.* Depressed, he slouched in his leather seat.

What he needed to bring his spirits up and get his creative mind flowing was to eat something rare, bloody, and juicy. His stomach rumbled in agreement. One last check on his patient, some instructions with the night staff, and umbrella in hand lest the light mist outside turn his blow-dried mane into a snarly mess, he headed off on foot for a nearby restaurant.

The motorcycle he had spotted on security cameras, which he assumed belonged to Clarice, no longer sat parked in his spot, a spot he rarely used given its exposure to the elements. He wondered if she'd discovered anything during her interviews. *Can she find the patients and prevent more loss of life?* Would her skills make a difference in the hunt?

At times like these, he wondered at the life of an agent versus that of a healer. Sure, they both had their versions of excitement, but while his kept him cooped up in one place solving medical mysteries, the other, field duty, meant getting out and about, having adventures instead of patching up the results. He couldn't help but remember the fun he had when he went with Mason to track down Viktor and Renee. Sure, he went in the capacity of a doctor, equipped to mete out medical aid if required, but he also recalled the excitement of tracking through the woods, of being on the hunt, a real hunt. Doing something outside the sanitized world he usually played in. Oddly enough, he wouldn't mind going on that kind of excursion again.

As if FUC would use him in a capacity other than that of a doctor.

As if his mother would let him.

As if he'd listen.

Maybe he should ask Kloe if any of the search teams would mind bringing him along. Despite his lack of field training, he did have a great nose. And given what they faced, his medical expertise, not to mention his giant kitty side, could come in handy. Something to ponder. After he ate, of course.

The barely singed, thirty-two ounce porterhouse served with two baked potatoes, salad, bacon wrapped scallops, fried garlic mushrooms, and aged red wine lifted his spirits a little. The tiramisu, fluffy sweet perfection, brought a smile to his lips. Leaving a hefty tip, Nolan walked back to the safe house to pick up his car, and that was when the back of his neck started to itch. Either someone followed him or he'd caught fleas again. Given he'd just had his mane groomed and kept up to date on his shots, the latter seemed unlikely.

Slowing his pace, he turned halfway as if to peer in a storefront window. In reality, he flicked a glance behind him. However, too many people milled on this stretch of sidewalk rife with fashionable boutiques and cafes for him to confirm his paranoia. Probably just a bunch of drunken secretaries again, trailing him at a distance, giggling. It happened more often than he wanted to admit.

Straightening his already impeccable tie, he took off again, sauntering as if he didn't have a care in the world, whistling a jaunty air, smiling at the ladies, and tipping an imaginary hat. As the traffic thinned near the brownstone and the buildings tapered from business to more residential, he gave no warning and darted into a shadowed space between two buildings, flattening himself against the wall.

Footsteps pounded on the pavement. He waited until the person, with no heed to stealth, flew around the edge into the alley. Quickly, he grabbed his pursuer and slammed him up against the brick wall.

"Why are you following me?" Nolan showed some teeth as he snarled in a most menacing fashion.

"Don't eat me. I'm a FUC agent," squeaked his follower.

"Eat?" Nolan wrinkled his nose. "That's even more offensive than the cologne you're wearing. Really, Old Spice? What are you, fifty?"

Actually, the young fellow shadowing him probably wasn't even legal to drink. "It's my father's, sir. I mean, doctor, um, sir."

"Let's stick with Dr. Manners and an explanation of why you're following me, and not very well, I might add."

"It was the office's idea."

"Office, as in FUC?"

"Yessir, um, Dr. Manners."

"And exactly what are you supposed to accomplish? Or let me guess. For some reason they pulled you from you regular job working…"

"In the mail room."

"To follow me around in order to what? Make yourself bait? Try my patience? Make the humans suspicious?" With each rebuke, the young shifter slumped. Nolan sighed and let him go. "Boy, you are much too young and ill equipped for this type of work. Much as I appreciate the concern of my coworkers, if I spotted you so easily, then anyone shadowing me would as well. I'd hate to see you come to harm. Go home."

"But—"

"Go home. I'll call the office and let them know. And next time they want you to play bodyguard or field agent, insist they pair you with a senior operative so you can at least learn the basics."

The young pup, a water mammal judging by his scent, probably on loan for an internship, scampered off and Nolan shook his head. What a joke. Sure, he wasn't the handiest of men when it came to battle, or so he let people assume, but still… A wet behind the ears teenager to guard him? Even his littlest sister could have kicked his ass. Hmm. Bad comparison. Even when kitten-sized, his youngest sister was a vicious, spitting thing.

Whipping out his cell phone, Nolan dialed as he resumed walking toward the parking garage where he kept his car stashed, not trusting to leave it parked on the street, even though he had a designated spot.

Kloe answered on the second ring. "Nolan. I take it you're calling me to inform me our latest patient expired?"

"No, although I expect it to happen before morning. I'm actually calling for another reason. I have a complaint about your choice of shadows. Is the boy even legal to drive?

"Are you speaking of Ethan, the otter?"

"An otter? Really? You do realize I am a lion, as in king of the jungle."

"Not the concrete jungle."

"Perhaps not, but still more capable than that teenager you sent."

"I am going to assume you spotted him."

"Spotted and sent him home before he missed his bedtime. I don't need a babysitter."

"I didn't think so either, however, several of our other agents were concerned about your well being given the threats made to you by some of the patients."

"While I appreciate the concern, I think I'd rather take my chances on my own."

"I don't know if that's wise."

"Are you aware of something I'm not?"

Kloe didn't immediately reply.

"Don't make me call my mother."

He could almost see his boss shudder. The last time his mother thought her baby boy was in danger, she raised holy hell at the highest level. Everyone at FUC heard the roar.

"Please don't."

"Then talk." Not his proudest moment using the threat of his mama to get info, but hey, it worked.

"There's been another killing by what we suspect is an escaped patient."

"And?"

"And it was one of the nurses. Agnes."

Nolan stumbled to a stop, his shock and grief at her passing instant and genuine. Poor aging Agnes. Set to retire just next year and gentle as a lamb. "Not Agnes. That's horrible. But how did they find her?"

"We're still trying to piece that together. We think it's possible one of the escaped experiments followed her from the safe house. I was going to wait until morning to tell you, but I guess there's no point in delaying now. We're shutting that location down. It's too compromised."

"So where are we going to bring the patients when we recapture them?"

"Nowhere. Capturing is off the menu." Kloe went silent after her low pronouncement, and Nolan growled.

"Oh no, don't tell me you're listening to that bird-brained female and Viktor. We can't just execute them. It's not their fault."

"Nolan. Agnes isn't the only one. We've got one other shifter in severe condition after an attack by what they termed a monster, and several humans missing with witnesses claiming a giant blob took them. We can't hide from the truth. The escapees are killing shifters and humans. They're compromising us all. It's out of my hands now. The orders have come down. We are to use deadly force. We're no longer out to capture."

"You're going to execute them in cold blood?"

"It's for the best."

"I see." He didn't. But then again, he thought of poor Agnes and the other victims, and could understand their reasoning. He just didn't have to like it. Nolan scrubbed his face before asking, "So where will I be working?"

"For now, in the FUC offices. We need all the help we can get."

I wanted to help, but not like this. Not because people are dying. "I'm a doctor, not a detective." Funny how he argued and yet, not even an hour ago, he wished he could do more.

"A doctor who might see things we missed. We could use your help, Nolan."

Help in killing patients he'd failed to heal? He squeezed the bridge of his nose. "I want it noted that I disagree with the termination order."

"Already done."

"I need my own space."

"We'll manage something."

"Then I'll see you in the morning."

"Um, since I've got you on the line, I don't suppose you could come out to the crime scene tonight, before we clean it up for the human authorities. While we didn't make it to the human attack or injured shifter one, we're currently in control of the crime scene for your former nurse. Can you come?"

Now, before he'd had his after dinner nap? Darn it. The things he did for work. "Very well. Give me the address."

Kloe rattled it off and he punched it into his phone's Google Map. Location saved, he ended the call as he entered the dark parking garage. His footsteps echoed loudly in the cavernous space, the dim lights, spaced far apart, doing little to illuminate the darkness. At this hour, most of the spots were empty, but the lingering scent of car exhaust, oil, and gas still perfumed the air, masking other scents, the one drawback to the location. It occurred to him that anyone could hide amongst the fat pillars and shadows. He peered around him suspiciously, but his lion sense remained quiet. Danger didn't lurk. Or so his inner feline assured.

Pulling his fob from his pocket, he clicked it once and the lights on his car flashed just as he heard the scuff of feet behind him.

Not again. Nolan whirled around to chastise the otter pup who'd obviously not given up when something dropped on him from above, bashing him in the skull and giving him the nap he'd so ardently desired.

Chapter Four

Driving a motorcycle gave Clarice a great feeling of exhilaration. It didn't compare to flying, but when the wind streamed through her hair as she poured on the speed, it came close. However, driving a sports bike came with drawbacks. A prime example was exiting the restaurant—chosen because it looked like a greasy spoon that knew how to serve a proper home cooked fry—to find it gone.

"Are you freaking kidding me?" She planted her hands on her hips and surveyed the parking lot. Full of motorcycles, hogs for the most part, her crotch rocket should have proven safe amongst the bigger bikes. Or stood out because of its difference. Whatever the case, she currently found herself minus a means of transportation, which was of course when she got the call that they required her presence at a crime scene. To make her evening complete, she dug a hand in her pocket only to realize she didn't have enough cash to taxi over.

"I hate the city!" She shook a fist at the blinking neon lights, but it didn't bring back her precious. Nor did she have time to hunt the perpetrator down. But she'd be back, and when she did…

Grumbling about the scum of humanity, she hiked the mile or so back to the brownstone only to discover the place practically deserted as a FUC cleaning crew cleared it out. Her fault because she'd argued with Kloe it was compromised. Apparently, she'd argued too late given one of the staff already ended up a victim.

Walking up to a woman with a clipboard, Clarice flashed her credentials. "ASS Agent Tertius on loan to FUC. Have you evacuated all the daytime staff?"

"Yes, ma'am. And the nighttime staff were given the evening off with strict instructions to safeguard themselves and call if they spot anything suspicious."

"You haven't noticed any lurkers?"

"No. Nor is this van going anywhere where more shifters will be compromised. We're just ensuring the records are cleared out, then boxing them into a storage unit until we deem it safe to move them to a secured FUC location."

"What about the moving staff themselves?"

A smile with too many teeth met her inquiry. "We know how to lose a tail. Don't worry about us."

"I guess you've got things under control then."

"Yup." The broad in charge didn't even lift her head as she kept checking off her list.

Snob. Clarice slinked off, not about to ask her for bus money because then she might have to admit she'd gotten her bike stolen. Spotting a bus stop with one of the nurses she'd interviewed earlier standing around waiting, she sauntered over.

"Shouldn't you have gotten a ride with one of the agents?" she asked.

"I'm not going home. I'm taking this to the airport, then I'm going to visit my sister."

Good plan since the patients wouldn't have the ID required to make it past airport security.

"Do you know if this bus will take me into the east end of the city?"

"What happened to your motorcycle?"

Refraining herself from scuffing her foot and ducking her head in shame, she instead replied, "I'd rather not say."

"Let me guess, you stopped in at the Hungry Heifer."

"Maybe."

The nurse laughed, but not in derision. "Someone borrowed your bike, I take it?"

"Maybe." Clarice shifted from foot to foot.

"Happens all the time. Those biker guys don't like to share their space with crotch rockets."

"So I've learned. I don't suppose you have a spare bus token I can borrow."

"I do, but why would you take transit when you can probably hop a ride with Dr.

Manners? I just saw him a few minutes ago. If you hurry, you should still be able to catch him. He's parked in the garage over there."

Bum a ride from the spoiled cat?

"What's he drive?"

"An Audi A4."

Oh sweet heaven. Clarice might have wet her panties a little at the news. Screw pride and screw public transit. She wasn't about to miss a chance to ride in luxury. *I wonder if he'd let me drive?*

Waving goodbye and wishing the nurse luck, Clarice jogged in the direction the lady pointed. Her soft-soled leather boots didn't make much sound on the pavement; as such, she managed to sneak up to within a few hundred feet of the oblivious doctor striding to his car when a shadow detached from the ceiling and dropped on him.

And she meant dropped. Down he went, like Michael Bisping when he got KO'd in the fight with Dan Henderson. Not even thinking, Clarice pulled her gun from the holster under her arm and took aim. Lucky for the idiot who attacked Sylvester, she didn't immediately shoot, more because she didn't want to deal with the paperwork if she inadvertently winged the FUC doctor, thus she heard the ensuing baffling conversation as a second shadow emerged from behind a cement pillar.

"What the hell, Betty!"

"Did I kill him?" Betty asked as she got up off the ground, brushing off her ample bottom. Poor Nolan lay prone on the ground. Given the weight that landed on him, he'd wake with a headache at the very least, if not a few broken ribs.

"Gosh, I hope not. That would totally mess up the plan, not to mention his mother would murder us."

"Murder? You didn't mention she had homicidal tendencies when you roped me in, Susan."

"Well, it's never been proven she killed anyone." Betty sighed in relief, but her friend Susan wasn't done. "But I have heard tales about torture. I heard the last person to hurt one of her family suffered for days. They say she clawed them to ribbons."

"Wish my mother was that tough," grumbled Betty.

"Don't we all." Susan knelt by the doctor and peeled back an eyelid. "What did you hit him that hard for anyway?"

"I didn't mean to. I meant to land on his back. I kind of missed."

"I'll say, and I thought the plan was to fall in his arms."

"I panicked. I didn't want to smash my face on the pavement."

"You're a cat," snorted her friend with disgust. "We land on our feet."

"Not always," grumbled Betty.

"Now how are we supposed to get him back to our place?"

"Stuff him in the trunk?"

"Oh yeah, because nothing screams, 'Hey baby, wanna screw?' like being locked in a confined space."

Clarice, listening to this, became more and more confused, but not worried. The idiot pair had yet to notice her skulking closer, and from their conversation, it was clear while their intentions weren't entirely aboveboard, neither did they seem homicidal.

"Fine. Forget the trunk. We'll stick him in the backseat."

"And if he wakes up? I don't want to be driving around with a pissed off lion in the back."

Planting her hands on her hips, the chubby one with a fear of hurting her face snapped. "I'm open to your brilliant idea then. Oh, that's right, you don't have one."

"It was my idea to waylay him after work."

"And that's worked out sooooo well," Betty drawled.

"Not my fault someone won't leave the donuts alone."

"It's genetic."

"Says the girl with a pantry full of sugar."

Betty stuck out her tongue and Susan shook her head. "We don't have time for this. We really should get him out of here before someone comes along. Give me a hand." Susan heaved open the Audi's rear passenger door before bending down to grab Nolan's enormous loafer-covered feet.

"I'll help, but don't think I'm forgetting you called me fat," Betty replied with a scowl. She grabbed the feline's other end and heaved.

Having heard enough, Clarice strode forward, gun still pointed. "Halt in the name of FUC and ASS."

"What?" Susan dropped his feet with a *thunk*.

"I think she said fuck him up the ass," whispered the chubby one, her eyes riveted on Clarice, or more accurately, the gun.

Stupid agency acronyms, they couldn't come up with something cool like the humans' FBI or CIA? "Put the lion down," yelled Clarice.

"This is none of your business. Just walk away."

"Says the stupid one to the lady with the gun." Clarice shook her head. "Okay, you idiots, I'm going to say this slow since it's obvious years of bleaching and cosmetics have burnt what common sense and intelligence you both were born with. Put the lion down. He's not going with you. He needs to come with me."

"We found him first," Susan said with a stubborn tilt of her hips.

"Yeah, finders keepers," Betty added.

Clarice pulled back the hammer and aimed. "I've had a trying day, bitches. The kind of day where I'd prefer to shoot, dump your bodies, and pretend I never saw you so I can get to where I need to be. Who wants to die first?"

"Die? Over a lion." Down thumped Nolan's head as Betty let go of her prize. "This is getting way too dramatic, even for me."

"Ah, come on, Betty. The chick is bluffing."

"Am I?" Clarice cocked her head.

"Yeah, I think you are." Susan grabbed his feet and hoisted them again. "Besides, we more or less have permission."

"To kidnap?"

"His mother promised a place in her pride to whoever could seduce her son and produce her first grand cub. She didn't say he had to be willing. Grab him, Betty." Gnawing her lower lip, the friend did as told and they toted the doctor a few feet.

The explanation just about rendered Clarice cross-eyed as she tried to follow the illogic. She gave up and fired a shot, the cracking sound loud in the cavernous parking lot.

Susan squeaked. "Are you crazy?"

"Crazier than a loon. Now drop the lion."

"Have it your way." Susan let go.

"To think I shaved my legs for him." Betty dropped her end and Nolan's head hit the pavement for the third time that evening with a thump.

With a disdainful sniff, the incompetent kidnapping duo stalked off, high heels clacking, and in the chubby one's case, wobbling.

Clarice sighed as she tucked her gun away. What had she just gotten involved in? Some kind of family politics from the sound of it. Not her problem. She had more pressing concerns such as getting to the crime scene, but first she needed to haul an unconscious male lion, who weighed way more than his appearance indicated, into the cramped back seat of his Audi. Unlike the two felines, she didn't fear him waking up any time soon, not with his triple concussion, but just in case, she used his silk tie to bind his hands. Then she hopped behind the wheel of sinful speed only to realize she'd forgotten to search him for keys. Sprawled lengthwise across the back seat, she had to frisk his lean length, scrounging in his pockets, feeling muscled thighs before she located his fob. If she inadvertently groped another part of his anatomy that even at rest proved the old adage big hands, big feet…then it was entirely accidental. Really, it was.

She started the car. The turbo-charged, direct-injected, two-hundred-eleven horsepower engine started with a sweet rumble. Clarice just about pulled a chicken, or in fowl terms, almost laid an egg in excitement. Now here was a purr she could learn to love. Windows down, music blasting, and hand on the shifter, she flew on wings of rubber.

Whee!

*

Nolan woke to a throbbing in his head, which didn't improve when the bed he snoozed upon suddenly swerved and he rolled into a tight space. His face smashed against smooth leather.

What the hell?

Struggling to roll back, he rested his bound hands on his stomach and blinked through blond lashes at the roof of his car. *How did I get here?* Last thing he remembered, a sack of bricks dropped on him a moment before he smelled tiger. But it sure wasn't a tigress who currently drove his car or whose scent lingered all over him.

Nope, that belonged to the woman with the straight black hair, the one who perturbed him, and whom if scent could be believed, groped his poor, defenseless body. Just what happened while he lay unconscious? And why did his head hurt so much? Only one way to find out. "This might be a stupid question, but why are you driving my car?"

"Awake finally, Sylvester? About time. Nap often on the pavement?"

"Only when attacked."

"By women." Clarice sounded amused. "You know, for a lion, you're not all that impressive."

"Says the woman who has yet to see me without my pants."

She coughed. "And intends to keep it that way. And what does penis size have to do with letting a woman get the drop on you?"

"You would have preferred I beat the woman up?"

"No. But you didn't even know she or her friend were there. If I hadn't come along, you'd have woken up tied to a bed somewhere as some kind of sex slave."

"Yeah. I wish they'd stop doing that."

The car swerved for a moment when Clarice swiveled her head to shoot him a shocked look. "You mean it's happened before?"

"More often that I'd like to admit."

Through the rear view mirror, he could see her gnawing her lower lip as she struggled not to ask. Turned out they had more in common than originally imagined because just like a cat, she lost the battle to curiosity. "I probably don't want to ask this, but why?"

"Could it wait until you've unbound my hands and let me out of the back seat? This isn't the most comfortable place." The backseats of Audi A4s were built for purses and really small people, not six-foot-plus male lions. "Which reminds me, why am I tied up?"

"I wasn't sure what kind of mood to expect when you woke up. I took precautions. I prefer to keep my head on my shoulders, thank you very much."

"I thought you didn't fear me?"

"Yeah, well, even the gentlest of kittens has claws, and I like my hair this length."

"I prefer to confine my scratching to the bedroom and be the cause, not the source."

"Too much info. And I guess given you're back to flirting, that answers my question of 'are you alright?' "

"Actually, other than a bit of a headache, I feel pretty good. I needed a siesta."

"You're now making me wish I'd left you on the ground."

"I'm sorry, did I forget to say thank you for rescuing me and putting me to bed? Or should you thank me because if I weren't here then that would mean you're stealing my car instead of chauffeuring me in it while I napped?"

Clarice snorted. "Only you, Sylvester, would call a concussion a nap."

"My name is Nolan, chicken hawk."

"I'm a falcon."

"Oops. Did I mention I'm also bad with names?" He tossed her a benign smile when she scowled. Two could play at her game. "So, where are we going?"

"Crime scene."

"Ah yes. Poor Agnes." His enjoyment at her discomfiture evaporated at the reminder.

"You knew her?"

"Yes. A lovely woman. I'm going to miss her. But I have to ask, why are we going together? Didn't you have a motorcycle? Don't tell me you left it behind."

"Not exactly. I seem to have temporarily misplaced it."

Laughter barked forth from him at her expense. "You went to the Hungry Heifer, didn't you?"

"How does everyone know that?"

"Because they're notorious for looking like a biker joint."

"Maybe because it has motorcycles parked across the front."

"Ah, but those are gang member bikes. And you are not a member."

"So I learned."

"Don't worry. I'll get the bike back."

"And exactly how will you do that, doc? I can't exactly picture you facing a motorcycle gang down."

"I have my sources," he replied enigmatically. "Now, do you mind stopping for a moment and untying my hands?"

"Stop? I'm kind of in a hurry and we're almost there."

The wicked bird. She meant to have him show up at the crime scene with his hands tied. Unacceptable. Nolan would never live it down, especially if Mason lurked. Damned bear had a way of always managing to pop up during a man's most embarrassing moments, then never letting anyone forget it. He also tended to take pictures.

Eyeing the knot, Nolan decided it would take too much effort to gnaw, so with a shrug, he flexed and pulled, tearing the silken tie, trying not to think of how much the darned thing cost. Hands free, he sat up and lounged in the back, the image of insouciance, an expression he suspected drove his avian chauffeur crazy judging by the scowl she shot him through the rear view mirror.

"Much better," he said. "Next time you tie me up, though, you should really try something a little tougher, say like handcuffs or nylon rope. I've got some if you need to borrow them."

"There won't be a next time."

"You say that now, but wait until you see the four posters on my bed."

"Let's get one thing straight, cat. I will never see the inside of your bedroom. You and I will never have sex. Flirting with me is a waste of precious oxygen."

"So you keep intimating, but our friendship is still young. I may grow on you."

"Like fungus? Doubtful. There're creams for that."

"Why are you so determined to dislike me?" Because despite himself, he found it harder and harder to muster the same feeling for her. Insults aside, she fascinated him. She didn't fall at his feet batting her lashes, yet he could smell her interest, see how her eyes tracked his every motion. She denied her attraction to him. How novel…and challenging.

"I don't dislike you."

"Liar."

"Okay, maybe a little. But if it's any consolation, I hate all felines on principle. It's how I was raised."

"I can understand an instinctual hatred of the uninformed of my species, those who haven't achieved sentience like a shifter. But to despise an entire species just because, doesn't that seem a tad unfair?"

"Cats eat birds. Or are you going to tell me you stick only to red meat that runs around on four legs?"

A sheepish shrug went with the lilt of his lips. "Touché. I'll grant you that I am not a saint when it comes to my meat dishes, but I'll have you know, not I or anyone in my family has ever eaten an avian shifter. We do have some lines we won't cross."

"Good to know."

"Although, if you'd be interested in a mutually pleasurable eating of certain body parts, I wouldn't be averse." Whoa, that was forward even for him.

"And this conversation is veering way off track." As if to punctuate her discomfort, Clarice poured on the gas. The car shot forward and executed a ninety-degree turn that sent him sliding. Bracing himself, he waited until she'd weaved through some traffic, without scratching his not-yet-paid-for Audi, before resuming the conversation on a different track.

"I see you know how to handle yourself behind the wheel. Did you have dreams of being a race car driver when young?"

"No, but I do love speed. Since I can't afford a beauty like this, I settled for a bike."

"You know, had I known you would be willing to drive while I slept, I would have offered you a lift."

"Luxury ride or not, I am not doing this because I want to. Stolen bike, remember?"

"I recall, and here I thought you followed me because you couldn't resist my charm."

"Anyone ever tell you that you're full of yourself?"

"Not exactly. Usually they're full of me and asking for more." No mistaking the high spots of color in her cheeks or the subtle musky scent signaling her interest—erotic interest. What he couldn't decipher was why it elated him. She still wasn't his type. Tell that to his stirring cock, though.

"You know, I'm beginning to wish I'd not interrupted those two broads accosting you," she snapped.

"Speaking of whom, I wonder who they were." A sniff of his clothing and he sighed. "The tigers again, I see. They really are persistent."

"So they weren't joking? They were trying to kidnap you to, uh—" The stain in her cheeks heightened.

"Seduce my body? Ravish me? Yes. They've been trying for months. My mother's promised a prize to whoever can present her with the first grandchild."

"You're kidding!"

"I wish. Since I wouldn't behave like a good lion of the pride and settle down with a harem of her choice, my mother took it upon herself to make me into somewhat of a challenge." Even thought he could only see her face from the side, he noticed how her jaw dropped. "Oh don't look so horrified. It has its advantages. I never pay for drinks anymore when I go out. Never lack for female companionship, and except for the occasional kidnapping attempt, have kept in shape evading the determined felines after me."

"And I thought I had problems," she muttered.

"It's not so bad. Those tigresses just caught me off guard." Probably because his mind was preoccupied with another female, but she didn't need to know that.

"Did I hear you correctly when you said you're expected to settle with a harem, as in more than one girl?"

"Again, my mother's old fashioned idea. She seems to think because I'm her only son that I should mate with a few ladies, spread my seed, and father as many cubs as possible."

"You don't sound like you agree."

"I don't. See, I'm also old fashioned. I told her I was waiting for love. Needless to say, that didn't go over well and has led to her increasing attempts at getting her way."

"That's sick."

"To an outsider, perhaps, but that's pride politics for you. Enough of my love life and mother, which I'm the first to admit should never belong together in the same sentence. Let's talk about you. Surely your mother has admonished you to settle down and nest or whatever it is you bird types do."

"One, I don't have a mother to bug me. And two, falcons mate for life. Something I'm not ready for." He heard the unspoken ever.

"No mother? Must be nice."

"Not really. Aerie orphanages aren't the nicest place to grow up."

Nolan wanted to punch himself when he realized how insensitive he sounded. He tried to apologize. "I didn't mean it that way. I mean, I'm sorry you lost your mom. It's just having spent my life trying to avoid mine, who is a tad too involved, it sounds kind of peaceful."

"Overbearing or not, at least you have someone looking out for you." And with that, she slammed to a stop, and having forgotten to put on a seat belt, Nolan's already sore head smacked into the back of the passenger seat. Ow.

Rubbing his forehead, he heard her exit his car without so much as a sorry, or a sympathetic look. How refreshing. He also got a great view of her butt, which filled out her pants quite pleasantly, but didn't entirely make up for her personality. Of all the women to get stuck with, he got the one who treated him as if he didn't matter. *I'm not asking for much. A kiss for my booboo. A come-hither smile. Her screaming my name, begging for more.* Given she never looked back, he doubted he'd get any of those things.

Lioning it up, he leaned between the seats, pulled a spare necktie from out of the glove box, wrapped it around his neck in record time, and departed his car to find himself in front of a trim bungalow. Single story, covered in faded yellow clapboard, where it lacked the white picket fence, scraggly boxwoods ringed the front yard instead.

Of Clarice, he didn't see a sign, but he did note the nondescript sedan in the driveway parked beside the VW bug, the daughter's car ,he presumed, the poor soul who'd found her mother's remains.

Assuming everyone was inside, Nolan followed the walkway, noting the missing heads on the towering sunflowers, the seeds scattered about on the cement slabs leading up to the front door. Given it was already slightly ajar, he didn't bother to knock.

Upon entering the tidy home, Agnes' familiar scent enveloped him, and a pang of sadness struck. What a shame about her untimely demise. He had quite liked the older matron, who despite her toad heritage and trademark croaky voice, treated him like a normal human being——and made the best cookies. At least by moving the operation from the brownstone, they hopefully wouldn't have to worry about any other of his staff becoming victims of the patients on the loose.

In search of Clarice and the other FUC agents, he stuck his head through an archway and noted a simply furnished, yet comfortable-looking living room with a worn, flower patterned sofa and an armchair whose headrest bore a crocheted doily. Nobody here. He kept going up the hall to where he could hear the murmur of voices and from whence wafted the coppery stench of blood.

Nothing could have prepared him for what he found in the kitchen. "Good grief, what happened here?"

Eyes dark and her lips twisted in anger, Clarice turned to face him. "Seriously? What's it look like happened, Sylvester?"

"Looks like a travesty," he moaned as he took in the blood-splattered walls along with the chunks of meat and bone tossed about the place.

The FUC agent, a snake by the name of Peter, looked a little greener than usual. He also held a big handkerchief up to his red nose. He sniffled wetly, and Nolan held in a shudder of distaste. Someone obviously had a cold.

The agent shook his head sadly. "Hey, doc. Thanks for coming."

"Of course. I came as soon as I got the call." Nolan ignored Clarice's derisive sound.

Sweeping out his hands, Peter wheezed as he said, "This is what the daughter found when she came looking for her mother. Needless to say, she's hysterical. Can't say as I blame her. Who would do such a horrible thing?"

"I don't know, but they definitely need lessons in taste. Don't they know HP sauce should never be used as a dipping sauce? The shame of it," Nolan lamented.

"Doc!" Clarice's blue eyes widened along with Peter's.

"What? What's the problem?" Nolan truly didn't understand their horror.

"This is a crime scene. Have a little respect."

"Yes, it's a crime, a crime to coat perfectly good buffalo ribs with an over the counter steak sauce. Or am I the only one with a sense of smell here?"

Peter sniffled. "I have a cold and can't smell a thing."

And Clarice, as a bird, possessed a poor sense of smell to begin with. But Nolan couldn't resist bugging them a little. "Oh come on, don't tell me you all actually thought these hunks of beef belonged to Agnes?"

Judging by the shifting eyes and feet, they did. Nolan, however, a great weight easing from his shoulders, smiled. Clarice peered around and even knelt to the floor to turn over a hunk of flesh with the bone still attached. She snorted. "Dammit. The cat might have gone about saying it wrong, but he's right. These aren't human remains."

"But the blood…the mess…" Peter pointed to the splatters.

"Barbecue sauce and rib juice. By all appearances, Agnes brought home some meat from the butcher." Nolan pointed to the stained brown paper under the kitchen table. "For whatever reason, she stepped out and someone broke in. Someone hungry and with no table manners." He sniffed and frowned. Many odors crowded the space; serpentine, amphibian, buttery popcorn, his own, and Clarice's, but under all that, he sensed another. The alien musk held hints of familiarity, but at the same time, seemed wrong. Very wrong to his finely tuned olfactory ability. "I can't be sure, but judging by the odd scent, I'll wager it was one of our escaped patients. For whatever reason, whoever broke in had themselves a feast, or a food fight. Whatever they did, they sure left a mess."

"Which the daughter came across when she popped in to visit her mother."

"Where is the daughter?" Nolan asked.

"In the bedroom. We thought it best to remove her from the scene of the crime."

"Someone needs to tell her the good news." Given the way Peter and Clarice feigned interest in the walls and floor, it seemed clear who they thought should get the job. *Well, at least I have something positive to relay.* Nolan headed back out to the hall and after a little searching, found a closed door from whence came soft sobbing. He walked in and found a slightly younger version of Agnes sniffling on a bed covered in a flowered quilt.

"I'm sorry, I didn't get your name from the FUC agent outside, but I'm Dr. Manners."

"A doctor? Fat lot of good that does with my mother in—in—pieces," wailed Agnes' daughter with a bullfrog bellow.

"Yes, about that mess you found. False alarm. Your mother isn't dead."

"Not dead?" The daughter blinked her large, bulbous eyes. "But I saw the body."

"No, you saw chunks of meat. However, they don't belong to your mother. Now…" He paused as if prompting her.

"Patricia."

"Lovely name, Patricia." He poured on the charm and she relaxed, even giving him a tremulous smile in reply. "Let me ask, do you have a cell phone, Patricia?"

"Yes. Of course. Why?"

"Please dial your mother."

As if on autopilot, Agnes' daughter pulled out her cellphone and hit a button. Nolan heard it ring once, then twice before Agnes answered with her customary brusque, "What?"

"Mother! Where the hell are you?" croaked Patricia.

"Having a beer at the tavern, why?"

"You're in a bar?"

"Ain't I allowed a drink?"

"But we were supposed to have dinner."

"Tomorrow."

"No, today."

"No, tomorrow. I have it marked on my calendar."

When it looked like Patricia would keep arguing, Nolan held out his hand. "Do you mind if I speak to your mother for a moment?" Patricia slapped the device into his hand, her tears completely dry, her lips pursed in annoyance with her no longer dead mother. "Agnes, this is Dr. Manners. So sorry to disturb you."

"Dr. Manners? Why are you on Patricia's phone? What are you doing with my daughter? Or should I say, what have you done? My Patty is a good girl. I won't have you breaking her heart."

Casting a glance over at the now simmering Patricia with her frizzy hair, sallow complexion and thin-lipped scowl, he held in a shudder. "I assure you, it's not what you think. It seems there was bit of a mix up at your house. Someone broke in and made a bit of a mess, scaring your lovely daughter."

"Is she okay?" Matronly concern overlaid her previous, suspicious tone.

"She's fine, just a little shaken up, but happy to know you're safe. She had a bit of scare when she came over and found your kitchen in a mess. We all had a bit of a fright until we determined you weren't harmed."

A long-suffering sigh left the matron. "Oh bloody hell. I'll never hear the end of it. I take it whatever mess is in my house will be cleaned by FUC?"

"I'll make sure of it myself."

"See if you can't get them to paint while you're at it. I hate the peach-colored walls. Something in a soothing mauve would be nice."

"I'll see what I can do. Needless to say, we're going to need you to stay somewhere else for a while."

"Is it the…" Agnes lowered her voice. "Patients?"

"Yes, I fear. Somehow, one of them found your home. We're going to need you to lay low for a while."

"Not a problem. I'll bunk with Patty at our summer cottage. No one knows where that is."

"Excellent. We'll have your daughter pack you a bag and someone will escort her home to ensure she's not followed so she can pack one for herself. The agent will then rendezvous with you and take you both to your cottage and remain until we can be sure of your safety. We want to take every precaution."

"Thank you, doctor."

Hanging up with Agnes after a few more words, he gave instructions to Patricia, who recovered quickly and simpered at him in a way that might leave lasting scars. Bulbous, lashless eyes should not blink so rapidly.

When the wet behind the ears otter shadow from earlier arrived—his need to ride the bus delaying him despite Nolan's orders he go home—Nolan sent him off with Patricia in her VW, holding in a grin. The poor lad. When Patricia latched on to the young man, he sent Nolan a terrified look over his shoulder. Nolan smiled and waved. The young fellow had wanted someone to guard. Being the magnanimous sort, Nolan gave him his wish.

Whistling, he returned to the kitchen to find Clarice handing off a Ziplock bag to Peter who already held a half dozen. "Find anything useful?"

"Some hair that I think belongs to our perp."

"Patient," Nolan corrected by rote.

A *humph* was her reply. "I've also got a hunk of meat with some teeth marks. The bottle of sauce with what appears to be a fingerprint. And a few other things for the lab to test."

"Fantastic. We can compare those items to what I have on file and hopefully figure out just who and what we're dealing with." Nolan already had a sneaky suspicion, but it never hurt to make certain. "Well, since you have things under control here, I think I'll be heading off."

"Off where?" Clarice asked, raising her head and pinning him with a stare.

"To bed, of course."

"Alone?"

"Despite my mother's wishes? Yes, alone. Unless you're hinting for an invitation to sleep over?"

"In your dreams, doc." Clarice stood and peeled off her latex gloves.

"Hmm, now that opens up a whole world of possibilities. I always did have a very active imagination."

Peter stumbled as he headed out of the kitchen with the evidence.

Pretending not to notice Clarice's dark glare, Nolan studied the crime scene and waited for her next repartee. To his chagrin, she didn't rise to his bait.

"I think you should stay with a friend tonight."

"Why Clarice, are you encouraging me to have sex? I thought you didn't approve."

"I said stay with a friend, not screw them."

"Doesn't that defeat the whole purpose of a sleepover?"

"Oh come on, don't tell me you've never bunked on a buddy's couch."

Actually, he hadn't. Home schooled and over protected, Nolan had very few friends to begin with, and of the male ones, none close enough for him to call out of the blue and ask such a large favor. Not that he'd admit it out loud. "I'd rather sleep in my own bed, thank you. It's been a rather long day and I am tired not having had my regular naps."

Hand sweeping out to encompass the messy kitchen, Clarice shook her head. "Going home is not a good idea, or is this not evidence enough that your home is probably not safe?"

"My building has security. I highly doubt whoever did this would have the same ease infiltrating my condo. Not to mention, I am a lion. I can defend myself."

Clarice arched a brow. "Yeah. I've seen how good you are at that."

Point for the bird. "Those tigers caught me by surprise."

"Exactly my point."

"It won't happen again. I'm more worried about my staff. People like Agnes who are not natural born predators. What's being done to protect them?"

"I already thought of that. I contacted Kloe. She's sent as many agents as she can to cover the houses of your staff, or at least those with some ability to defend themselves. Those most at risk have already been told to stay with friends or relatives until we can ascertain whether they are safe or not."

"Good. I'd hate anybody to get injured. Seems like you've got everything under control, so if that's all…" He yawned, stretching his jaw wide.

"You won't give in, will you?"

"Nope."

A long-suffering sigh escaped her. "I should let you go by yourself. It would serve you right if you got eaten."

"But?"

"But, it would look bad on my service record. Thanks a lot for leaving me no choice. Let's go, Sylvester."

"I thought we'd gotten past the name calling."

"Not when you act like that idiot cat on TV."

"I resent that. I don't lisp."

"Keep talking like an idiot and you'll sing soprano."

"Testy. Testy. See what happens when you don't take time for a nap?"

"The things I do for ASS," she muttered.

"Is that what this is about? You can have my ass anytime, unless you mean literally. I'm not into that kind of kink."

"I think fatigue is making you stupid. ASS as in… You know what, forget it. Just get your hairy carcass in the car so I can drive you home. I wouldn't want you to fall asleep behind the wheel."

"Liar. You just want to drive my car again."

A hint of a smile curled her lips, and it struck Nolan how pretty she looked. "It is a sweet ride. But, no, this has more to do with making sure your stupid feline butt doesn't get taken off guard by one of the psychos."

"Patients."

"Whatever. Let's go."

Leaving Peter to direct as the three-shifter-strong cleaning crew arrived, Nolan followed the bossy bird out to his car. It occurred to him for a moment to argue that he should be the one driving his car. But, the lure of a nap appealed more. And besides, he quite enjoyed her rigid annoyance when he used her thigh as a pillow. He enjoyed even more the scent of her musk enveloping him as he breathed against her.

Her body, willing or not, liked him, now he just needed to work on her mind.

Chapter Five

Watching from a few houses down, he couldn't hear what they said, but he saw the doctor exit the house of that nurse. How disappointing to find no one at home. But then again, he'd never enjoyed frog legs, even when cooked. The ribs helped with some of his hunger, but lacked a certain *liveliness* to them.

Eyeing the doctor and his female friend, he'd bet they'd taste much yummier. Even better than popcorn, but not possible for the moment. Off they zoomed in a fancy car. *I used to have a nice car like that once upon a time. And a handsome face.*

Until Mastermind stole it all.

He didn't know what irked more, the fact he hungered no matter how much or what he ate, or discovering Mastermind was already dead, which meant he wouldn't get the revenge he dreamed of.

Robbed! Robbed of a chance for vengeance. What was he to do? Someone had to pay. Someone owed him for the travesty done to his life and once beautiful face. If he couldn't kill the culprit then he needed to go after the source. Science. Science was to blame for what befell him. Science and doctors who thought nothing of playing God with people like him.

Kill all the doctors and there'd be no more victims. Stupid medical practitioners, thought they knew it all and flaunted their status every chance they got. Just look at Dr. Manners with his fancy car and good-looking girlfriend. He was the one who let Mastermind get to him. He was the one who failed to cure. The one who still had it all while he was forced to scrounge for scraps and hide in shadows.

No more.

He'd found the nurse easily enough via the Internet from the phone he stole. He'd find the good doctor as well. Find him. Punish him. Eat him. And then take what he deserved.

Right after he found some more popcorn. Those darned ribs he ate dipped in HP sauce weren't sitting well in his poor distended tummy. Oops. Not in his tummy anymore. Someone would get a surprise when they got up in the morning.

Chapter Six

Clarice couldn't help but glance with irritation—and bemusement—at the golden-haired male using her lap as a pillow. *This is definitely a first.* The guys she knew would never have dared such a liberty—except for a certain drunken dodo. Clarice's demeanor didn't invite snuggling. It didn't stop the lion from plopping his head down and going to sleep. And snoring! Not loudly, but enough to give him his first physical flaw—other than his species—which served to make him more human. Even—*ack!*—likable. It didn't mean she'd changed her mind about him. She wouldn't date or have sex with him, and she still thought him an idiot, albeit a good-looking one. She blamed the fact she found him attractive for her involuntary reaction to his presence.

The man drove her insane with his flirting, and despite knowing she shouldn't take it seriously, her body—to her extreme annoyance—reacted each and every time. One smile and her nipples hardened. A rumble of his voice and her sex clenched. The warmth of his breath against her crotch as he snored softly in her lap and she creamed her panties.

The smart thing to do? Shove him off her lap. Use her as a pillow indeed. Yet, for some reason, she did nothing, because to take offense would force her to admit he disturbed her. And she wouldn't give him the satisfaction. Now, if he went for a grope, that would put a different spin on things. An actual sexual advance meant she could freely give him the black eye he deserved. *Or I could grope him back.* Treacherous mind, or should she say body. What was it about this doctor that made her want to break her own rules?

She fought to change her train of thought and focused instead on the case, more specifically the danger Nolan kept denying. These *things* they hunted, by invading the home of a FUC staff member, showed a level of cunning. It disturbed her to realize they'd focused their rage on specific people and not just random strangers. But try getting an arrogant lion to recognize that. For a smart man, he could prove dense at times.

Obviously, the idiot didn't take his own safety seriously, and the more he claimed he could take care of himself, the more she wondered. Just look at how those tigers took him by surprise in the parking garage. Where did his king of the jungle instinct hide then? Deny it all he wanted, he'd not suspected a thing, yet, at the same time, even she had to admit, the tigers posed no real danger. If one ignored the concussion and the whole kidnap him for sex thing, the only real danger was to his virtue. *As if he had much of that to start with.*

Why his slutty behavior with the opposite sex made her grip the steering wheel tight enough to leave claw marks, she couldn't have said. She forced herself to relax and breathe. *I am not jealous. Why should I care who he sleeps with?*

And how had she digressed from her main topic of thought, mainly his ability to care for himself? As he'd evidenced, when he ripped the bonds binding his hands, he possessed strength, and by his own words, escaped more than one sticky situation. However, evading the amorous advances of the ladies was a far cry from escaping the not so tender, psycho tendencies of mutant killers. *What would the doctor do if faced with a former patient out for blood?* Would he do what it took to protect himself, or get himself killed trying to save someone too far gone to help? Somehow, she feared the latter, which she could grudgingly admit was not a huge flaw, just a possible fatal one. *Which is why I'm driving him home and letting him use me as a pillow instead of dumping his ass on the curb and taking off for my hotel.*

While his ability to defend himself remained unknown, Clarice already knew he wasn't as dumb as she'd initially thought. Oh, he seemed to enjoy giving the impression he was a golden playboy lacking common sense, and yet, he had immediately spotted what she'd missed at the crime scene. It didn't matter she would have quickly figured it out, and he, in a sense, cheated because of his refined sense of smell. Clarice jumped to the wrong conclusion and he proved her wrong. Again. An annoying habit of his she was quickly coming to hate. Now, if only she could hate the man instead of fighting an urge to brush a stray golden lock fallen across his cheek.

As she drove, fast—just because she really did love his car—she reported in to Kloe, giving her the latest the developments on the case.

The giraffe went silent when she was done. "So you're with Dr. Manners now?"

"Yes. When he wouldn't take my warnings seriously, I judged it best if someone competent attended him."

"He insisted on going home?"

"Yes, despite my recommendation. Would you prefer I take him elsewhere?"

"No actually. This might work for the best. Peter called after you left and said they did discover one thing missing when they packed up some stuff for Agnes. The nurses contact sheet, which she kept on her fridge, is missing."

"Let me guess. She had all the staff's information on it."

"No addresses, but phone numbers of some key staff members, which anyone with access to the Internet can use to do a reverse four-one-one. Good news is, we've already called them all and warned them so none of them are at home except for—"

"One stubborn kitty."

"Yes. But that might not be a bad thing."

"You're going to use him as bait?"

"If the doctor won't budge, then yes," Kloe said, bluntly.

"Won't his family, more specifically his mother, who I've heard is a bit meddlesome, take issue with that?"

"Probably. But at the same time, if someone messes with her little boy, then the pride will get involved."

"Get involved as in?"

"Hunt the patients down to make sure their only male lion is protected. If there's one thing you don't do, it's mess with Brenda Manners' son."

"So you want me to dump him in his apartment and hope he doesn't sleep through an attack by one of the psychos?"

"Not exactly. We'd like you stay with him for the time being, or until the danger has passed."

The car swerved. "What?" Clarice screeched. Stay with the overgrown kitty? Forced to endure more of his sly innuendos and his tingling touches? Oh, that was such a bad idea. Bad, bad idea. *And yet, wasn't I planning to spend the night?* One night. Kloe, on the other hand, implied longer.

"I am not a babysitter."

"I realize that. But even you admitted he couldn't be left alone."

"Because he's oblivious and more concerned with fixing them and won't admit they're a menace that needs eliminating."

"I don't have any other agents to spare, and you're already with him."

"Not by choice."

"Will you do it for tonight at least?"

"He's annoying." And sexy.

"Really? I'm surprised to hear you say that. The women around here love him."

"Because they want to do him."

"And you don't?"

"No," she lied. She refused to admit she had anything in common with those stupid hormonal females who fluttered their lashes. Yes, maybe she felt an urge to see if his golden flesh covered his entire body and if he sported fur on his chest, but she could live with that curiosity. No way would she allow him to ruffle her feathers and get close enough to purr against her naked skin. *Uh-oh, I shouldn't have thought about him naked.* She squirmed and his head lolled. He didn't wake up, but his nose ended up buried a little more intimately than she liked—okay, she liked, but wished she didn't.

Kloe still spoke and she struggled to pay attention. "I'm actually happy to hear he does nothing for you. Poor Nolan takes the overtures of the staff pretty well, but I know it wears on him."

"Sure it does." She'd seen how it bothered him in the way he kept inviting her into his bed.

"So I can count on you to keep him from getting hurt?"

Reluctance colored her reply. "I guess. But what about my things?"

"I'll have someone run you over some stuff in the morning."

Hanging up, Clarice glared down at the lion snoring in her lap. Less than twenty-four hours she'd known him and already he complicated her life. Boy, would she give ASS a good verbal spanking over this one.

Arriving at his condo, his car's GPS guiding her through the unfamiliar streets, she parked underground, some kind of transmitter automatically opening the secured garage. Given his address placed him on the top floor, it wasn't hard to guess which prime empty parking spot belonged to him. The big sign boldly stating, "Reserved for Doctor Manners" also helped.

Engine ticking, she sat for a moment staring down at his golden crown. Damned cat, he slumbered in her lap, an overgrown pet, unaware of the turmoil he caused. It didn't exactly boost her ego to know he could sleep so soundly after all his comments. Then again, given she didn't want his amorous attention, she should count herself lucky.

Still, though, it was with no little amount of irritation she shook him awake. Apparently, lions took their sweet time waking up. First, he groaned. Then stretched. He turned to snuggle deeper into her lap, his warm breath pulsing against her crotch, a heat felt even through her jeans. She couldn't help the pooling moisture when he purred, "Mmm, smells good," in a rough, sleepy voice. Oh yeah, she experienced a definite quiver.

Appalled at her body's reaction, and even more worried he'd notice, she shoved him off her lap by scrambling out of the car, leaving his head to thump on the vacated seat. Rolling over, he opened his eyes to pin her with an amused golden gaze and a rumbled, "Good evening."

"Not really."

"Not a night person, are you?"

"Not all of us have had time to nap."

"I'm more than willing to donate my thighs for your head if you feel a need."

"No, thank you."

"That's probably for the best. I don't think it would make the softest pillow."

Surely he wasn't implying… As he clambered out of the car, lanky limbs and all, she took a peek down. Oh yes, he did mean what he said, and sizably too. She quickly looked away, but he still chuckled, having caught her.

"Thanks for the drive and the pillow."

"Whatever. Are you coming?"

"Depends on you."

"I meant to the elevator."

"You going to see me to my door?" His lazy smile did strange things to her tummy.

Flustered, she looked away and headed to the elevators. She jabbed at the button before she replied. "How many rooms do you have?"

"It's a one-bedroom with a den. I went for a large, open space concept. Why?"

"How's your couch?"

"Large, but my bed is bigger. I assume you're asking this because you're planning on staying?"

"Just for the night. Since you refuse to go somewhere and there's no one else to spare, I get the lovely job of babysitting your hairy arse."

"Hairy? I'll have you know I have smooth cheeks. I can show you if you'd like."

"No, thank you."

"Are you sure? My back is hairless as well, although, I do have to admit to a bit of fur on the chest."

His admission had her eyes crossing as she imagined her fingers running through it. "I don't want to see any part of you unclothed, nor do I care if you require epilation on certain body parts."

"Shave my fur? Perish the thought. What about you?"

"What about me?" she asked.

"Is your butt hairy?"

The elevator door dinged and out she flew, her eyes scanning the short hall for intruders. Empty, she decided to reply and see if she couldn't throw him off balance for once. "I'm smooth all over. And I mean everywhere."

With that rejoinder, she grabbed his key from his hand while he stood, staring at her with a glazed expression. Was it wrong of her to preen now that she'd finally managed to best him?

Nah. As for the extra waggle in her walk? Birds strutted all the time, not just when they wanted to mate.

Opening the door, a carved wooden affair big enough to fit an elephant, she stepped into opulence.

"Holy pigeon poop!" To call his place nice would have proven the biggest understatement of the year. Other than the tile floor right when they walked in, the rest of the place boasted cream-colored carpeting—and not the cheap stuff. His wall-to-wall rug was thick, real thick. Kicking off her boots, she sank into it and bit back a groan of pleasure. Okay, so wealth did have some advantages, starting with the view any bird would kill for. Floor-to-ceiling windows overlooked the city where lights twinkled, keeping the darkness at bay. She pressed up against the glass, vertigo not an issue for obvious reasons. Now this was a view. A girl could make herself a cozy nest in a place such as this. With the right guy, of course, which the good doctor was most certainly not.

"I take it you approve of the scenery?"

"Maybe."

"Says the drooling birdie in my window."

"I am not drooling."

"If you say so. Oh, and just so you know, if you need a place to take flight from, there's a balcony in my bedroom."

Good to know for practical reasons. She'd have to check it out, and not because a part of her wondered about where the lion slept. Or if he kept track of his conquests on his bedposts.

"Hungry?"

It surprised her to realize she felt a tad peckish. Dinner digested hours ago, she couldn't quell the sudden rumble of her tummy, a sound he of course heard. A grin turned his sexy mien boyish.

"I'll take that as a yes. Let's go see what we can find in the fridge."

Following him through the impeccably clean space—that put her housekeeping skills to shame—she entered a kitchen dream, for someone who cooked.

Granite counters, stainless steel appliances, dark wooden cupboards—a modern culinary masterpiece. While she could admire it, she didn't covet it, not when her idea of cooking involved dialing the pizza parlor down the street, or picking up sushi on her way home.

"You handy in the kitchen?" she asked, propping her butt onto a high-seated barstool.

"Ha. As if my mother, my cousins, or my aunts would let me near their kitchen. Nope. My knowledge stops at the microwave."

A frown marred her face at the evidence of numerous sealed containers in his fridge. "You seem pretty well stocked for a guy who doesn't cook."

"The pride apparently fears I'll die of malnutrition. They make sure I always have meals handy, like premade sandwiches for the nights I work late." From one of his laden fridge shelves, he pulled a plate covered in clear wrap. But to call the masterpieces on the ceramic serving dish sandwiches did them a disservice. She counted at least six kinds of buns, in pairs, with green lettuce peeking from their middles. As to between the breaded halves? Ham and Swiss with Dijon mustard. Roast beef, mustard, and sharp cheddar cheese. Some kind of egg salad mix, which she avoided with a moue of distaste and which he sheepishly disposed of. A BLT on a sesame bun, which she devoured along with a tuna fish mayo blend that just about made her swoon, especially once she bit into it and noted they'd used real tuna and not the canned stuff.

Bottled water helped wash it down. Stomach appeased, she leaned back on the stool, feet hooked on the lower rung. "Spoiled much?"

The doctor lifted a shoulder. "I guess. It's not like I have much choice. I tell them there's no need to feed me. I am perfectly capable of calling for food or picking something up. They just ignore me and do what they want."

"*They* as in your family?"

"Yes. The pride takes care of its own."

What a novel idea. "What about when you get married? Or settle down with a *harem*?" She couldn't say the word without sneering.

"Oh, I imagine they'll back off a little, but short of moving far, far away, I doubt I'll ever convince my mother, or even my aunts for that matter, to ever completely leave me alone."

"Must be nice."

"Not really. These things come at a cost."

"So they charge you?"

"Not monetarily."

When he didn't expand, she held her tongue. The arrangement he had with the female members of his family didn't concern her. She could do nothing, however, to curb her envy. What would it be like to have someone care for her every need? To come home knowing she'd have something to eat? Someone who kept watch for her? Someone to guard her back? *Someone who loves me?*

She must have required more sleep than she initially thought to let something like a plateful of premade sandwiches launch her into such a maudlin state of mind. "We should hit the hay."

"I hope you don't mean that literally. I don't think we keep any grass or twigs around for nesting. Would blankets do?"

"Ha, ha, Sylvester. Don't give up your day job because your career as a comedian will prove short."

"I wasn't trying to be funny. Just trying to find out what you need to get comfortable."

"A blanket and pillow for yonder couch will work fine."

"Take the bed."

"No, thank you."

"I insist. I'll sleep on the couch."

Sleep in sheets imbued with his scent, possibly still carrying the scent—or icky stains—from his latest amorous encounter. No way, although given the cleanliness of the place, they were probably pristine. Still, though, she didn't need any more fodder for her surprisingly overactive imagination where he was concerned.

"You keep the bed. I wouldn't want you to end up sleep deprived."

"You know, we could share. It's big enough for two. Actually, we could comfortably fit more."

"Know that for a fact, do you?"

"Unfortunately, yes."

For some reason the thought he'd experienced what he pretty much admitted to an orgy prickled. Flicking her hair back, she stood and walked away. "Where's your bathroom?"

"Through the door with the frosted glass. Do you want something to change into? I don't have any woman's clothes, but I can offer a t-shirt or something."

"Nope. I'm good."

Given the opulence of the living room and kitchen, the marble garnished bathroom with its double sink, super-sized glass shower, and plush towels didn't surprise her in the least. Using the facilities, she took a moment after she washed her hands to splash her face with cool water, unable to avoid seeing her reflection in the mirror.

A familiar visage looked back. Not exactly pretty, or so numerous people remarked—some of them while dating her—with features too bold and sharp for cuteness. Still, though, she wasn't butt ugly. She possessed clear skin, lustrous hair, and straight teeth. But what did she care how she looked? It wasn't relevant to the job at hand.

Nolan thinks I'm sexy. Probably because she kept rejecting him. A man like him, used to women dropping their panties if he so much as smiled, probably thought her a challenge. And he could keep thinking that bccause she had no interest in bedding him. Nope. None. No matter how sexy he appeared when she stepped out to find him wearing low-hipped lounge pants and a form-fitting under armor shirt.

It took her a moment to register he held out an offering, more like waved it in her face. "Here. I know you said you didn't want one, but in case you change your mind, this should act as a nighty."

"Thanks." She grasped the offered t-shirt.

"I put some blankets and pillows on the couch. But again, if you find it too uncomfortable, the bed is big enough for two."

"No, it's probably best if I sleep out here, you know, in case of an attack."

"Right. So I guess I should say good night."

"Good night."

Why did they stand there staring at each other? Bodies swaying closer, as if pulled together by some invisible force. Her breathing shallow. His eyes dilating. The tip of her tongue darted out to moisten her lips. A rumble went through him. She snapped back.

What am I doing?

Without another word, she practically flew around him and dove onto the couch.

"I'll see you in the morning," he said gruffly.

Burrowing under a blanket, body hot, heart racing, she managed to mutter, "Yup." And then proceeded to toss and turn until dawn before falling into a restless sleep where she dreamt she was a giant yellow bird chased by a great big kitty. Only, when she was caught, the type of eating he put her through had her screaming in pleasure, not pain.

Chapter Seven

Falling asleep should have happened in seconds given the evening's activities and his snack. However, Nolan, arm cradled under his head, couldn't get his mind to shut down, not when he remained all too aware of the woman crashed on the couch just outside his room.

Clarice.

A bird.

A sexy chick.

A sexy, aggressive falcon who hated him because he was a lion. A spoiled, useless feline according to her. The knowledge she thought so little of him should have predisposed him into disliking her in return, or at the very least, allowed him to ignore her.

Nope.

Despite her angular frame, her snide remarks, the whole species thing, and more, he couldn't help a tug of attraction. More than tug, full-blown arousal. Just the mere thought of her had him tenting his covers. What a pain. Blue balls and Nolan weren't closely acquainted. Usually when he got a sexual urge, the reason for it was on hand—and sometimes knees—to take care of it. On rare occasions when he didn't feel like company, he let his hand do the work. Lying alone in his room, he couldn't bring himself to take care of his large problem. Nor could he saunter forth and pour on the charm in the hopes of a BJ or some action. From what he'd learned of Clarice so far, she was more likely to shoot him than give him sex.

I wonder why she's so prickly? Part of it stemmed from the whole avian versus feline problem. Instinct was a hard thing to fight, but he got the impression her aggressive nature went deeper than that. He sensed trust issues on her part, big ones, and suspected her attitude was her way of shielding herself from emotional damage. Could the loss of her mother explain it? What about her father? Where was he in all this? And why did his furry side think that licking her from head to toe would turn her prickly fowl temper into cooing erotic bliss?

Pondering the various ways to tame the wild bird on his couch followed him into sleep where he dreamed himself into a certain cartoon character on an endless chase after an elusive bird. Not exactly restful. Certainly not in the ordinary, and kind of disturbing given once he caught her and realized his comic book version didn't have the proper equipment to do what his mind fantasized.

While in the midst of that dilemma, a loud noise penetrated his dream and Nolan instantly woke. He flung the covers back just as his condo door slammed shut with a resounding boom. The snarled, "Who the hell are you?" by a voice he recognized—*uh oh, Mother's here*—followed by Clarice's belligerent, "What's it matter to you, cougar?" spelled an even bigger uh-oh.

"I'll ask the questions here, bird. Where's my son?"

"In the bedroom. I have to say, though, don't you think you're a little old for him, grandma." Crazy falcon. She baited the wrong person. Nolan couldn't help but grin, though, as he imagined his mother's face. *I am liking my new ASS friend more and more.*

"Grandma! Did you just call me old?"

"So sorry." Yeah, she didn't sound too apologetic. Nolan knew he should get out there, but a morbid fascination over how far Clarice would push his mother kept him still. Clarice didn't disappoint. "Would you prefer the term cougar? Cradle robber? Mrs. Robinson?"

"I am not here to sleep with him, hussy."

"I'm sure that's a first," Clarice replied. "And I wouldn't be tossing names, or did you not notice the fact I was sleeping on the couch until you barged in?"

"Obviously, he wanted to sleep alone. Yet, look at you. Desperate for attention, lounging on his couch, half-naked." Half-naked? Really? And he'd missed it. Damn. The mental image almost made him miss his mother's next words. "He's probably hiding in his room waiting for you to leave. Can't you take a hint? Get your clothes and go."

"Not happening."

"Excuse me. Do you know who you're dealing with?"

"I think I can guess and my answer is still no. Like it or not, I'm not going anywhere. As a matter of fact, you should get used to seeing me around. I'll be sticking real close to Nolan. And I mean *close*. Where he goes, I go."

Dead silence. "Are you implying what I think you are, big bird?"

"Big? I wouldn't be calling me fat, Garfield. Did someone indulge in one too many saucers of cream? You know, the pet store is having a sale on catnip and mice. Maybe you should invest in some and work off those extra pounds."

Enjoying himself way too much, Nolan didn't immediately get up, even when he heard the crash of what was probably the glass dish holding his keys. It wasn't often he got to hear someone stand up to his mother. Unless they possessed a death wish. He also found it interesting that despite Clarice's intentional misleading statements that she and Nolan were involved, he didn't bristle, sweat hairballs, and he didn't want to scale out his balcony window and run. Usually when a female got possessive, his first instinct involved extricating himself and hiding. However, in Clarice's case, even though said jokingly, her taunt of sticking to him like glue made his furry self purr and puff his chest. Had someone slipped him some catnip in the ventilation system again? Why on earth would the idea please him?

The melody of chaos continued via more taunting and thrown objects. God only knew the mess his mother made in her tantrum, a mess he most certainly would not clean up. When he heard the feline roar, though, which meant his mother shifted, he hopped out of bed, and clad only in his boxers, exited the bedroom.

Turned out, he needn't have worried. Despite the large lioness pacing his living room, teeth bared, hair hackled, and eyes glaring with hatred, Clarice didn't appear the least bit worried. Standing in a half crouch dressed in tight boy shorts and a sports bra, which showed off her tanned and muscled physique, Clarice stood before his transformed mother dangling a piece of string, cooing, "Here, kitty, kitty. Come and play. Someone needs the exercise before she gets too fat to chase mice."

Leaning against the doorjamb, Nolan shook his head, unable to stop his lips from curling. "You know, most people would call what you're doing suicidal."

"Bah. I think of it as exercise. Some people rely on a gym. I prefer real life to keep me in shape and on my toes." She reached out and tapped the enraged matriarch on the nose. Blinking and shaking her head, his mother snarled. Clarice, despite her human form, snarled back. Mother dear, not expecting the response, narrowed her gaze and crouched down for a pounce, long tail thrashing.

"Not in the house," he admonished.

"Yeah, chubby kitty. You heard the king of the jungle. No fighting in his house."

"Clarice." Nolan moaned her name, and not in a good way.

His mother coughed her displeasure.

Shaking a finger, Clarice tsked. "Bad kitty. No hacking up fur balls either. I hear they're hell on carpet."

The look on his mother's face? Yeah, Nolan didn't even bother fighting his erupting laughter. "Yup. You are definitely suicidal. When you're done playing with my mother, would you like some breakfast?"

"Are you cooking?"

"Are you insane? I've got room service on speed dial."

"You live in a condo, not a hotel," she replied as she dodged a swinging paw with claws protruding. Clarice retaliated by dangling the string and making kissy noises.

"A condo with many amenities. Any preferences for food? Actually, I'm famished this morning. I'll just get two of everything and you can choose what you want."

"Sounds good," Clarice said as she bounced up on his couch and then flipped over it to avoid his mother's lunge.

The chick had some moves, he'd give her that. And if he kept watching, he'd probably show some definite movement in a fashion that might prove embarrassing. Turning away from the action, he sauntered across the room, forgetting for a moment he only wore his underwear, but he remembered real quick at her sucked in breath. Turning his head, he caught Clarice's glazed expression, parted lips, and the tightening of her nipples through spandex fabric. He also saw his mother coil herself to spring while Clarice was distracted.

"Shit." Leaping across the room, he made it in time to knock his mother aside before she disemboweled his temporary ASS partner. Needless to say, that didn't go over well.

Changing shapes in the blink of an eye, his very naked mother—*Ack! I'm blind!*—hands planted on her hips, hollered at him, "Nolan Fitzgerald Benjamin Manners, you did not just attack me in defense of a bird."

"Benjamin?" Clarice snickered behind his back.

"Shut up, Tweety." He didn't flinch at the punch Clarice aimed at his kidneys, but he did at the narrowed lips and deadly expression in his mother's eyes. Uh-oh. Trouble. And before breakfast, too. He could already predict this would cut into his morning nap, or judging by the position of daylight across his floor, afternoon one.

"Is someone going to explain what is going on here?" his mother asked in a low voice.

He didn't immediately answer. Instead, grabbing an afghan from the top of his couch and tossing it his mother's way, said, "Mom. Please. I have a guest."

"You have a *bird* in your condo." How she made the word sound dirty, he couldn't have said, but he could feel Clarice bristling behind him, ready to begin round two of the taunting.

"Can this not wait until after breakfast? I'm hungry." He put on his best pout. Lower lip jutting, big eyes batting, and his mother, tying the blanket sarong style, not falling for it, at least clamped her mouth shut. Now if only he could duct tape Clarice's.

"You have got to be the biggest, laziest pussy I've ever met, Sylvester."

"Sylvester?" asked his mother in a choked voice.

Whirling, Nolan shook his finger at his ASS partner. "Stop that right now."

"Or you'll do what?"

He blurted the first thing that came to mind. "Kiss you."

"Excuse me?"

"You heard me. If you say one more thing to drive my mother mental, I will kiss you."

"You wouldn't dare."

"I would, with tongue too."

"In front of your mother?" Clarice moistened her lips.

"Yup."

"That's not fair. You know I don't like you."

"I think you protest too much. Is this your way of trying to force me to do it? You know, you could just ask. No need to play these games. I'm more than willing to kiss you."

"You're sick."

"So you keep saying."

Ignoring his mother's piqued interest, he held Clarice's gaze, hands on the back of the couch, leaning against it to hide the stirring interest from a certain body part. To his relief—and major disappointment—Clarice backed away, lips pressed tight as she grabbed her clothes, heading to the bathroom. One sniff, though, and Nolan could smell the interest she pretended didn't exist. He also scented the filth of the previous days excursions on the clothes she planned to wear.

Stepping in her path, he pulled the fabric from her hands. "Oh no you don't."

She tugged back. "I need to get dressed."

"Not in that you're not."

"Oh yes I am."

"Nope." He danced out of reach, Clarice hot on his heels. He dove into his room, hit the patio doors, and slid them open in one deft motion. Without pause, he flung her filthy things over the railing. Down they sailed. Clarice clasped the balcony railing and peered over the edge. He took a peek himself to see her garments sinking in the pool.

"Do you know how long those took me to break in?" she snapped.

"I'll have them dry cleaned and returned later. Now, why don't you go shower? You stink." He pinched his nose and held himself taut for the punch she aimed his way. Wow, she could pack a wallop. So, of course the side of him that apparently enjoyed abuse had to say, "Didn't hurt."

"I hate you."

"You know what they say about hate."

"I don't want to have sex with you."

"Who said anything about sex this time?"

With a growl, she whirled on her heel and stalked off. He grinned at her retreating back. "There's a robe hanging on the back of the bathroom door for when you're done," he mentioned as he followed.

She answered him with a flipped finger as she stalked past his mother, who watched with a calculating look. He whistled as he strolled to the phone and ordered enough food for a small army, then he headed into his bedroom as the shower turned on. Grabbing a t-shirt and track pants, he dressed quickly and exited to find his mother also attired once again, her outfit not the one she'd arrived in judging by the shredded remains of silk on the floor. He didn't bother to wonder where it came from. Given his mother's temper, he figured she had clothes stashed everywhere she went.

As he padded into the kitchen to get some coffee going, she followed. He was ready, more or less, for the interrogation he knew he couldn't avoid.

"Who is she?"

"A coworker." No, he wasn't going to make it easy on his mother, not after the way she behaved. Goaded or not, she should have shown a little more control.

"A coworker who spent the night in your condo in her underwear!"

"Well, yeah. We got in late and she didn't have any jammies. Would you have preferred to encounter her naked?" He certainly would have.

"You're being deliberately obtuse."

"How? I've answered your questions," he replied with a sly smirk.

His mother's lip tightened into a thin line. "I am going to ask once again, and you better answer me straight this time, Nolan. Who is she and what is she doing here?"

"I'd say that was obvious. She's ASS and she was taking care of my body." At the sour expression on his mom's face, he couldn't help laughing. "Get your mind out of the gutter, Mother. She's ASS, as in Avian Soaring Security. Kloe assigned her as my bodyguard. We had some security concerns over those escaped patients so Clarice was asked to stay with me until another agent comes available."

Instantly, his mother's irritation switched to concern. "Are you in danger?"

He shrugged. "The agency seems to think so."

"Because he is." Clarice answered as she emerged from the steam-filled bathroom wearing his robe, which looked way too big on her slender frame. It made her appear cuddly, feminine, soft… Seeing her wear it, knowing it bore his scent, that the fabric had touched his skin, roused something primitive in him. A sense of possessiveness flooded him, a new feeling he'd never felt before for a woman, or at least never until Clarice. *Mine*. He swallowed hard and hoped the sensation would pass because despite his attraction to the falcon, getting involved would just invite trouble. Loads of it.

"I can't have my only male heir threatened. You will pack a bag and move in with the pride until the danger passes." His mother stated it as a done deal, however, Nolan wasn't about to let himself get sucked into his mother's clutches. No way. If he allowed that, he'd wake one morning to find himself wedded and bedded to who knew how many felines as part of his mother's political machinations.

"No, I'm not. I'm staying right here."

"Oh no you're not."

"Good luck convincing him otherwise," Clarice muttered as she prepared herself a cup of coffee—her eyes lighting with pleasure at the Keurig machine on his counter and the array of Kcup flavors.

"Why are you being so stubborn?" his mother asked.

Other than the fact he was a big boy who didn't want his mommy protecting him? "FUC needs me."

"No, we/they don't." Clarice and his mother spoke at the same time, and with the exception of one word, parroted each other. Not that they appreciated the fact their minds swung in the same direction judging by their matching glares.

"Yes, they do. I'm the one who knows my patients best. I can help. Not to mention, I make great bait."

"No son of mine is dangling himself in front of a bunch of crazed killers."

"Why not?" Clarice taunted. "Can't your boy take care of himself? Or does he need his mommy to fight his battles?"

Since when was his reluctant ASS partner on his side? He eyed her suspiciously, especially given her benign smile at his mother.

It was a nice play, though. Either his mother called him a pussy, or she had to admit he wasn't completely useless. In other words, it could go either way. Nolan wished he'd thought to put a shot of something alcoholic in his French Vanilla flavored coffee.

"Nolan is a perfectly fine fighter. He had nothing but the best teachers growing up. However, we're talking about homicidal maniacs. If half of what my sources tell me is true, then only an idiot would try and face these escaped abominations alone."

"He won't be alone."

"Why? Are you going to stay glued to his side and protect him? Ooh, I'm just shaking in my fur. What are you going to do, big bird? Shake your wings at the attackers? Regurgitate some worms and spit at them."

Clarice sighed. "What is it with you cats? You know, it's not all about hand-to-hand combat or animal shapes. We have evolved. There is such a thing as weapons nowadays."

His mother sniffed. "I should have known you were one of *those*."

"Why you catty b—"

"I smell breakfast!" Nolan announced, stepping between the brewing fight to answer the door. The catering staff wheeled in several white cloth-covered carts holding an array of covered dishes.

The presence of the human staff kept his mother and Clarice silent, but the visual daggers flew fast and furious as they each paced their end of the room.

As soon as the caterers left, with a generous tip in hand, Nolan seated himself and lifted the domes from the platters. Steam arose along with mouthwatering scents. "Time to sheathe the claws, ladies. Breakfast is served." Like naptime, Nolan let very little get in the way of his food. A lion needed to keep up his energy after all, especially when dealing with his mother. And, he amended, when juggling a ruffled bird who looked like she'd rather peck their eyes out than sit down and eat.

"We should be getting to work," Clarice admonished.

"Eat first," he ordered between mouthfuls.

"Let the bird go. I'll get you to the office," his mother offered.

Before he could refuse, Clarice replied, "On second thought, I am rather hungry. I guess catering to a male lion's *needs* will do that to a girl."

Nolan almost choked.

*

Barb thrown, Clarice tucked the robe around her, and ignoring the older cat's rumble of discontent, sat at the table. Truth was, she did feel rather famished this morning and despite her less than great sense of smell, even she couldn't resist the rich aromas wafting from the table. The doctor wasn't kidding when he said he would order everything on the menu. Waffles, big and fluffy decorated in whip cream poufs, a spattering of icing and fruit tempted on one dish. Toast towered. Pancakes steamed. Bacon from barely cooked to crisp, along with sausage and ham made her mouth water. Orange juice beckoned. Coffee promised a return to sanity.

"Where's the eggs?" his mother demanded.

"Out of deference to my guest, I didn't think it appropriate."

Ah, how sweet. Gag.

His mother couldn't leave it at that, though. "Afraid of eating a cousin?"

Clarice arched a brow. "Are you always this crass or did someone forget to take her meds this morning? I hear menopause can be rough on women your age." Target launched. And…boom. Direct hit. Fury had the woman red-faced and ready to lunge across the table.

Figured Sylvester would ruin her fun. "Enough. From both of you," Nolan ordered. "Mother, mind your manners, and you, Clarice, eat or I will make good on my promise from earlier."

A kiss if she didn't shut up? Damn, he needed to come up with a better punishment or else she would start trouble just to see if he'd follow through.

A silent, if uneasy truce descended as they ate, and ate, Clarice not even coming close to packing away as many calories as the two lions. Where did they put it all? She'd seen Nolan almost naked. The man, contrary to his lazy nature, didn't have an ounce of fat on his frame. Nope, all six-foot-plus of him was tanned, toned muscle with a layer of…

A knock sounded at the door and Clarice used it as an excuse to escape the erotic images determined to batter down the wall in her mind. She put her eye to the viewing hole and groaned.

Could she pretend their newest visitors weren't there? The knock came again in a quick, insistent patter.

Swinging open the door, Clarice stepped aside to let the visitors in. The annoying rabbit of the day before hopped in followed by her lumbering bear of a husband laden with some familiar luggage.

"Oh goody. I thought I smelled food." Off Miranda bounced to join the feast, going right for the carrot muffins, which along with several of the other healthier items, remained untouched.

"Morning," Chase said gruffly, dumping Clarice's bags at her feet. "Kloe asked us to bring your stuff. Apparently, my being a lawyer isn't an important enough job. FUC has relegated me to bellboy."

"Now, now, grumpy bear. We both know you cleared your client calendar, what with the baby coming soon and the whole crisis with FUC having everyone on edge."

"I cleared it so I could catch up on my sleep before the cub is born."

"Sleep? Who has time for sleep? There is still so much to do," Miranda reminded as she inhaled all the muffins and then started on the cheese Danishes, which resulted in a growling tugging match between her and Nolan as they fought over the last cherry one.

"I thought pregnancy would slow her down," Chase admitted mournfully as he sat in a chair and reached for a honey-glazed donut that wisely, no one contested.

"Oh pl—l—l—ease. I've never felt more energetic," Miranda drawled holding up the larger half of the pastry she'd won.

"I've noticed."

"How come no one's killed her yet?" Clarice whispered to Nolan. "This much cheerfulness is not normal."

"Believe me, lots have tried."

"I sense a *but*."

He shrugged. "Let's just say, Miranda's a lot tougher than she looks."

Carrot muffins demolished, Danishes conquered, and yogurt inhaled, the pregnant bunny patted her rotund belly. "So, what's the plan for today?"

"You are going to stay out of trouble," her husband warned.

Waving a hand in dismissal, Miranda didn't take offense. Did anything penetrate her cheerful veneer? "Of course I am. I was asking them what their plan was. I know I can't fight any bad guys until the baby is born."

"I don't actually know what the plan is," Nolan replied. "We had a late night and just got up."

"I do," his mother said. "He's coming with me and letting the pride protect him as my only male heir."

"Pussy," Chase coughed into his hand and Clarice snickered. Nolan did not look pleased.

"I am not going with you, Mother."

"What's ASS girl over here planning?" Miranda asked, nibbling on some fruit.

Take offense or not? Deciding it was too early in the day to pick a fight with a pregnant rabbit, Clarice let it slide. "I'm going to check out some other crime scenes."

"Hey, that sounds like fun. Mind if I come along?" Nolan perked up.

Her first impulse was to say no, but then she caught sight of his mother violently shaking her head and the fledgling inside her, who enjoyed irritating her elders, spoke before she could stop herself. "Sure, but only if I get to drive again."

"Again?" His mother's eyes almost fell out of her head. "You let her drive your car?"

"Twice. It's a sweet ride." She didn't feel a need to mention that the first time he did so unconscious in the back with his hands tied, or that during the second trip, he snored in her lap. Didn't matter, his mother appeared even more shocked than when she walked in and found Clarice standing in her underwear in the middle of the living room pointing a gun.

"Thanks a lot," Nolan muttered under his breath, which wasn't what brought a pink stain to her cheek. The squeeze to her thigh under the table managed that.

Clarice pinched him as Nolan's mother launched into another tirade, abetted by Clarice who couldn't help but taking the opposite stance of whatever she said, compounded by Miranda, who insisted on also taking Nolan's side, while Chase and the damned lion in question closed their eyes and napped.

In the end, Clarice won; Brenda, the pride matriarch, stormed out; Miranda, nose-twitching and eyes twinkling with mischief dragged away a half-awake bear with threats of shopping for a crib, and left her alone with a snoring Nolan.

"You can stop faking it, they're gone," she announced.

He cracked open an eye. "Thank God. I thought they'd never leave."

"Is it always this chaotic in the morning at your place?"

"Not usually. Mother pops in whenever she likes, but I tend not to have female guests over. I don't share the bed well."

"Says the man who kept offering me half of it last night."

"I would have made an exception for you."

"Lucky me."

"Yes, you are. I don't just let anyone sleep over."

"And yet, from the sounds of it, you entertain the ladies quite often. So what's the deal? You do them, then kick them to the curb?" Somehow, she didn't take him for the a-hole type. But apparently, she was wrong.

"No. That would be rude. I thank them very nicely for the evening, put them in cab—

which I pay for—and have them text me when they get home safe."

"That sounds kind of cold."

"Hey, I'm not the one seeking these women out. They're the ones who come after me. I just give them what they want."

"It still makes you a slut."

"I prefer the term dutiful son."

"If you're so dutiful, how come you haven't popped out any babies yet for your mother to corrupt? Shooting blanks?"

He snorted. "No. I'm a big believer in covering my soldier."

"Soldier?"

"He conquers only when covered in armor. Extra-large armor, I might add." With a sinful smile and a waggle of his brows, Nolan rose from the table, and with his hips swinging his ass in a way she found much too riveting, left the room—but not her mind.

Heart aflutter, probably from all the cholesterol she inhaled for breakfast, Clarice couldn't help but watch. Despite her decision to dislike him, the cat was getting under her feathers. Stupid her, though, she'd finagled a day spent in his presence. Maybe she'd get lucky and Kloe would get her out of it. She called her boss while the water ran in the bathroom.

"ASS Agent Tertius reporting," she announced when Kloe, who refused to respond to a proper title, answered.

"Ah, Clarice. I wondered when you'd call. I take it you got my messages."

"Messages? What messages?" Pulling her cell from her ear, she peeked at the screen and noted the voicemail icon lit up. She must have missed the calls during the brawl with his mother.

"Doesn't matter now that I have you on the line. I know your plan was to check out some of the locations where we've had reports of sightings."

"Yes, ma'am."

"Kloe."

She held in a sigh. "Yes, Kloe. I'm hoping to find some clues as to where the killers are hiding."

"I pray you have luck. We need to stop them before there are any more fatalities, or worse, the wrong people notice them. We're extending all of our resources trying to keep this under wraps. I fear it blowing up in our face if we don't find them soon."

"I'm on it." Or would be as soon as she got off the phone and finished dressing.

"Now, usually, I would never do this, but I'm finding myself in a quandary with all of our current FUC agents scattered around the city on assignments of their own, which is why we want you to take Dr. Nolan with you. We know he's not the ideal partner for a hunt of this kind, given his medical training, but we don't want you investigating alone."

Not ideal was an understatement. "Too late."

"What do you mean?"

"It means I already told him he could come," she admitted, if begrudgingly.

"Oh how excellent. I am glad to hear you're getting along so well, that makes my next request easier. Given again the whole tapped resources thing, we'll need you to remain glued by his side until the missing patients are caught."

"What?" Never mind she'd antagonized his mother claiming she planned to stick to him, she'd never actually meant it. "I thought you were going to try and have me replaced with someone else."

"Unfortunately, we have no one else. Or no one with enough skill to actually protect him."

"I'm not a bodyguard."

"No one is asking you to be one. We simply want an extra set of eyes and defense in case someone comes after him. Since you're already working together and I can't spare anyone else, then I see no reason to change things up, unless there's a problem?"

A problem, like the fact she wanted to peck his eyes out half the time and the other half she wanted to molt in his arms? She gritted her teeth. "No problem. I'll keep the furball out of trouble."

"Excellent. Well, then, I guess I should let you go. If I'm not mistaken, I hear my next appointment." Judging by the roar Clarice faintly heard through the receiver, she could guess who it might be. *At least I won't be the only one dealing with an annoying pussy today.*

Hanging up, she dug through the bag Miranda brought and pulled out some clothes. Dressed, she paced the sunshine-filled living room, forced to wait while Nolan did God knew what in his bedroom. Whatever it was, it involved a long shower, some blow drying, and whistling. By the time he emerged, she was ready to pluck his hair out one strand at a time.

"Ready to go?" he asked.

"I've been ready for over half an hour," she snapped.

"Well, excuse me. I had business to tend to."

"I don't call blow drying and hair conditioning business."

"Says the woman with split ends." His rueful headshake did nothing to improve her mood, but she also couldn't help sneaking a peek at the ends of her hair as she followed him out of the apartment.

Down the elevator they rode, her in simmering silence, him with a half-smile on his lips as he hummed.

When they entered the parking garage, she noted a gorgeous Goldwing parked alongside his Audi. Her eyes lit up with avarice. Sure, she loved a sport bike with its speed and sleekness, but compared to the behemoth before her with its eighteen hundred horsepower and all the bells and whistles? It was the Cadillac of bikes when it came to comfort and power.

"Like it?" Nolan purred from behind her.

"Who wouldn't?"

"Good. It's ours for as long as we need it."

She whirled. "Seriously? But why? How?"

He shrugged. "I felt kind of bad you lost your motorcycle yesterday. I made a few calls to some friends of mine at the precinct, but according to them, it's probably already being shipped overseas or in pieces being sold for parts. So I called a buddy of mine at a dealership and had him send this over."

"This is what you were doing while I was waiting?"

"In between blow drying and curling? Yes." His eyes twinkled with mirth. "I needed the extra hair care given what the wind and helmet will probably do to my golden locks."

No, she wouldn't melt. Wouldn't melt. Wouldn't…ah, damn it all. He made it hard to remain angry, especially when sinful temptation sat waiting for her. "I'm driving," she stated.

"You know, traditionally, the woman sits on the back." He laughed at the dark glare she shot him. "But I guess there's nothing traditional about the pair of us. So long as you don't mind if I have a nap, then she's all yours."

All hers. Hmmm, funny how when he said that, it wasn't the bike she pictured, but him, between her thighs, two hundred plus pounds of pulsing power… She shook her head and grabbed the helmet hanging off the handlebars. She jammed it on her head, but ignored the goggles. No need for those.

Nolan wrinkled his nose before gingerly placing his own headgear atop his pride and joy. Add a pair of aviator glasses and the lion looked hot. Real hot.

She turned her back to him and straddled the bike, heaving it upright. "Get on," she ordered. The beauty of a Goldwing all decked out? It was a bike designed for two.

Despite having his own seat and armrests, Nolan still placed his hands on her waist, making her all too aware of him behind her. He leaned against her back and purred. "I'm ready to ride."

Mmm, judging by the moist heat between her thighs, so was she. She kicked the stand up and cranked the throttle. Then, on two wheels, away they flew.

Better than sex and almost better than flight, Clarice reveled in the wind blowing in her face, the power between her legs, the male wrapped around her back. He leaned into her, probably napping again, which was why she didn't make an issue of the hands that slid from her waist to thighs.

Using the most amazing GPS system built into the Goldwing's dash, they easily made it to the overpass Jessie advised them to check out first. Close to some of the sightings, and a popular gathering spot for transients, it seemed a likely hidey-hole for some of their escapees. Gliding to a stop, she took a moment to examine the scene.

Immediately, her sixth sense kicked in and warned her of danger. Her rapier gaze took in the deserted campsite made up of forlorn tents, boxes, and mussed sleeping bags, but no signs of life.

Nolan growled softly. "I smell blood."

"Awake, Sylvester?"

"Who says I napped?" The hands on her thighs squeezed, shooting a spurt of warmth to her mound.

"Oh yeah, if you were so awake, then what's the drool on my back from?"

Flicking the kickstand in place, she slid out of his grasp off the bike as he sputtered, "I do not drool."

"If you say so. Come on, helmet hair, I want to get a closer peek." She grinned as he cursed. Too easy. Striding closer to the abandoned transient village, her gaze zeroed in on the brownish stains dotting the ground. She dropped to her knees and touched them. Mostly dry, which made them several hours old at the very least. "These aren't fresh, but I wouldn't peg them as older than a day. Can you smell anything?"

All jocularity and sleep disappeared from his visage as Nolan took on a predatory cast, his lean body coiled as he prowled the area, sniffing and crouching for a closer perusal. When he got like this, she couldn't help but admire, even covet him. Why he hid this male under his playboy persona she didn't understand. Then again, maybe she did. If he had a hard time beating off the ladies as a foppish mama's boy, imagine the troubles he'd have if they knew those mannerisms hid a strong and able male.

"I scent two, maybe three shifters. Recently too." He inhaled deep and coughed. "Definitely ours. I recognize one of the odors."

"Which one?"

"The cat, Beverly was her name. Shy and a tiny little thing. Or she was. The other one could be Leroy, also one of our patients, one of the unknowns."

"Could be?"

"There's something off about the smell. Almost as if he's sick."

"You can tell that by smell?

"It's not hard really. A body that is in ill health tries to eject the toxins poisoning it. Very distinctive, trust me."

"And the third scent?"

"Again, probably one of the patients, but I couldn't tell you for sure which one. It's really messed up." His nose wrinkled.

Crab walking, Clarice moved over to a mound of something ooey and gooey. It didn't appear healthy, or of natural origin. She grabbed a stick off the ground and poked at it. "What the hell is this?"

"Gross."

She shot him a dirty look. "I can see that, but I asked if you knew what it was. This isn't human or animal in origin. It's too jellylike."

"Maybe it's hospital gelatin gone bad." He shrugged. "I'm not a walking encyclopedia, you know."

"And here I thought you had an answer for everything."

"I'm glad to see you think so highly of me."

He would take it as a compliment. "Idiot."

"Are we back to the name calling?"

Ignoring him, she stood and scouted the area, trying to piece together what happened. Signs of a struggle littered a few spots: torn sleeping bag, overturned cart with belongings strewn, an ear. Hmmm, which reminded her to ask, "What of the humans who lived here? What do you smell? In other words, do you think they're dead or alive?"

Standing and wiping his hands on his jeans, Nolan sighed. "Probably dead. Their corpses, or pieces of, are somewhere around here, I'll wager. I can smell the beginning stages of rot."

Kind of what she figured given the abandoned area. Having once lived on the streets when she ran away from the aerie orphanage, she well knew how the homeless treasured their belongings. No way had they abandoned their stuff.

"So where are the bodies?"

He pointed at a fabric lump down a ways, and to brownish stains over the concrete barrier meant to keep people from accidentally falling in the river. Clarice wandered over to peek over the edge, which plunged about fifteen or twenty feet to the murky, sluggishly moving water. Hanging half-in, half-out of the stagnant river, caught on a metal grill, was part of a corpse.

She'd have to call in a cleanup crew. No way would human authorities miss the obvious gnawing and chunks of missing flesh. She took a stroll amidst the makeshift camp. A few more body parts hidden amidst the detritus showed up on her search, but not enough to account for the number of people she would have assumed lived here.

"That can't be all of them." A camp this size with a prime location under the bridge would have had at least half dozen or more. Clarice planted her hands on her hips as she peered around.

"Not unless they ate them."

"Out in the open? They're crazy, but not completely oblivious." Not if they'd managed to evade them for so long. "They obviously took the bodies somewhere else to cannibalize. But where?"

Nolan paced under the bridge, the sun not quite penetrating the depths of the arch, but illuminating enough for them to see the metal service door inset in the wall, its lock busted.

Damn, she was hoping his nose would lead him away from the dark, enclosed space.

"Where do you think that goes?"

"Sewer system and the storm drains. City workers need a way to access them. Looks like the ones we're tracking might have dragged their victims inside."

Figured. Why couldn't the hunt have involved a sunny, flower-filled field? Moaning about it wouldn't change anything. Clarice slapped away her annoyance and prepared to brave the dark. "Stay here while I take a look."

"You are not going in there alone." He crossed his arms and his lips pulled into a stubborn line.

"I won't go far. Just enough to see if you're right about them having gone to ground."

"They have."

"It won't hurt to check."

"You know what Kloe said. No confronting any of them without a full team."

"We don't even know if they're in there."

"Oh, there's at least one, maybe more. I'm calling for backup."

"So quickly? What happened to giving them the benefit of the doubt? Saving their souls?"

If possible, his face turned grimmer. "I changed my mind. It's too dangerous."

"Pussy."

"Is everything a challenge with you?"

She answered honestly. "Yes. Now are you going to get out of my way so I can do my job or not?"

"I forbid it."

She choked. "You forbid it? Oh that's funny."

"I am not joking, Clarice. You are not going in there. It's too dangerous."

Hot as she found his newfound backbone, she also wasn't about to give in to his orders. He didn't own her. No man did. "This is what I do, doctor. I investigate dangerous shit. It's why I carry a gun." She patted her holster. "Now get out of my way before I make you cry for your mother."

"You know, you keep assuming you can take me."

"Because I know I can."

"Don't be so sure. I'm not as useless as you think."

"Says the man with more hair products than a beauty salon."

"Just because I take care of myself doesn't—you know what? I give up. You want to go in the nasty, dark sewer, then fine, be my guest, but I'm coming with you."

What made him change his mind? Her brow creased. "I thought you wanted to call for backup?"

"I've already texted the office. They're sending a team."

Sly kitty. She'd not even noted his flying fingers, too intent on their verbal sparring. She really needed to up her game around him. "Excellent. Well, if help is on the way, then what are we waiting for?"

"Sanity."

"Way overrated." Clarice pulled out her gun, one of them at least. "Where's your weapon?"

He arched a golden brow. "I don't need one."

She clucked her tongue. "Such a man thing to say. Stick behind me. I don't care how big these psychos are, it only takes one well placed bullet to stop even the largest animal in its tracks."

"Don't count on it," he muttered, but he didn't impede her as she stepped through the door into a small, closet-sized room with a hole in the floor. The ladder bolted to its side headed ominously down.

Even her meager sense of smell twitched with discomfort at the miasma wafting up. Perhaps this wasn't such a good idea. She didn't even have a flashlight, or…

A click and a feeble bulb encased in a metal cage lit up inside the hole. It didn't improve the appearance of the ladder leading into the sewer.

"At least the electricity still works," he announced.

"Yay." Her enthusiasm emerged flat.

"Are you sure you want to do this?" he asked softly. "We can turn back."

The sense of danger prickled at her from all directions, a warning she should heed, urging her to head for the skies. To open space. Anywhere but here. She almost turned around. Almost. But she wasn't a weak fledgling, the orphanage made sure of that. She straightened her spine, hardened her resolve, and mustered her courage. "I'm sure. Let's go."

And down she went into the bowels of hell, also known as every toilet in the city.

Chapter Eight

Nolan could have shaken Clarice for her stubborn refusal to wait for backup. As it stood, he almost tossed her over his shoulder and dragged her away. However, he knew it would do no good. Not to mention might have ended up with someone getting hurt—more than likely him.

Despite only knowing her a short time, he understood enough to realize Clarice wouldn't back down. Something in her past made her feel like she needed to prove herself. Forced her to do the opposite of what common sense dictated. Short of knocking her out, she was going to explore the damned sewer. But she wouldn't go alone.

Nose twitching, stomach not happy, and his lion senses tingling, he followed. Danger lurked below. Waited. Watched. Nolan might not have the experience of his jungle cousins, but he retained enough of his heritage in his genes to know when something stalked him. It oddly enough roused the hunter in him, the beast who didn't appreciate the fact something considered him prey. Even odder, his bestial side was angered at the thought something watched and hungered for the woman he followed into darkness.

More and more, he couldn't deny his growing regard for Clarice. He could blame it on their forced proximity. Relegate it to his cat's curious nature, which wanted to know why she wouldn't succumb to his advances even though he could smell her desire for him. Despite the vast differences between them, it wasn't one-sided. Awareness sizzled whenever they got close. And if he were quite truthful, she fascinated him. Drew him. Enthralled him like no other. He'd never before wanted to get to know a woman like he wanted to know her, and not just know her in a carnal way, but in every sense, from her favorite color and movie down to the taste of her skin, and if she possessed ticklish toes.

Her prickly exterior didn't scare him off as she intended. Her anger and insults rolled off his furry skin. He could see underneath all the posturing lurked a woman looking for acceptance. A vulnerable woman who needed love, which he was sure she'd vehemently deny, probably to the death—his death.

What to do? Standing in a rank sewer probably wasn't the time to ponder that question.

He took better stock of their location. The ladder had led them down to a rather cavernous room. Tunnels led off in all four directions of the compass. From the one to the east, the distinctive odor of malodorous river flowing under the bridge wafted. The cage-covered lights illuminated most of the path and daylight did the rest, if weakly, through the heavy grill plastered with debris, probably washed there from the last storm surge passing through.

In the other three directions resided the mysteries. He could see that the lights in the northern passage had burnt out in some spots and who knew what lurked in the side tunnels branching from it. The water running between the parallel walkway had only the most sluggish of currents. He couldn't tell how deep it went and really didn't want to find out.

To the west and south, something had deliberately ripped the lights out, the metal cages twisted and bent, some torn off entirely. Not an ounce of illumination gave any indication of what waited. But, his nose knew. It smelled the blood. The rot. The sense of *wrongness.*

Clarice rotated around slowly, pacing the area, taking the same visual inventory. A scuff from a side tunnel halted her and he almost stumbled into her back.

"We should leave."

"Scared, Sylvester?" she taunted in a low whisper.

"Nope, smart enough to know we are underequipped."

"I agree."

He almost fell over in shock. She agreed? Perhaps the fumes of the sewer were stronger than he realized.

"Let's go back topside and wait for the reinforcements to arrive."

Mark it on the calendar and declare a holiday. Clarice finally saw reason. Too bad it was too late.

*

Clarice regretted her decision to enter the sewer as soon as she hit the bottom of the ladder. *What was I thinking?* She was a falcon, meant for open spaces and the sky, not confined rooms underground where thick gloom hid everything. Her skin itched and crawled, and not just from the creep factor. The great bird in the sky only knew what germs this pest infested place held.

How she hated to admit she might have acted hasty, though. In her quest to prove herself bigger and better than the FUC agents, she'd done a dumb thing, one her magpie sergeant would have croaked about for days. She'd gone into uncharted territory with a rookie, underequipped, undermanned, and against a direct order that stated to proceed with caution and wait for backup. Not only that, she took along a lion who was barely a step above civilian. If SGT Noireau were here, he'd ream her feathery tail out and clip her wings for weeks.

But there was still time to rectify the mistake. She shoved Nolan at the ladder, but he had to turn all gallant and dodge out of the way. With sweeping hands, he said, "After you."

"This is not the time to act the gentleman."

"Who says I am?"

"Then you go first."

Again, he graced her with the smile that made her heart flutter faster. "And miss the opportunity to see your tight tush going up the ladder?"

The warmth his words sparked at the knowledge he found her attractive almost trumped that of the intrigue at making him go first so she could indulge in the same visual pleasure. The argument over who would go first, though, soon became moot as the metal hatch of the opening above them clanged closed, and more ominously, they heard a bolt sliding shut.

"Uh oh," she muttered, the claustrophobic feeling increasing.

"I think this is more of an 'oh shit!' moment," he added nudging her in the side. "Don't look now, but I think we have company."

Whirling, she didn't immediately see any approaching menace; the tunnels remained clear. "Where?"

"You need to look down. Check out the water."

Yup, I definitely should have stuck to open skies. The ominous ripple in the dirty murk moved with purpose toward them, and she could almost hear the theme to Jaws as it approached. Was it wrong to hope an overlarge rat left the wake? Or fish? Those she could handle. Heck, she'd eaten them raw for lunch in the field during her training. *But I doubt I'll be eating anything I find down here, especially considering anything living in here is probably a mutant.*

"What should we do?" whispered Nolan, his eyes fixed on the hump rising from the foul slime. Since running was out of the question, and she refused to scream like a girl, that left them only one real option.

"Sharpen your claws, Sylvester, because I think we're about to see if you're as good as you claim to be."

Gun in one hand, knife in the other, she braced herself. The ripples in the water flattened as whatever approached sank deeper in the sewage. Not exactly reassuring. Tense minutes passed. They waited. And waited, the only sound that of dripping water. *Plop. Plick. Plop. Plick.* Yawn.

Seriously? She shot a dark look at Nolan, who grinned sheepishly and shrugged. "What can I say, I'm bored."

She might have hissed a retort, but apparently, the waiting creature didn't like his comment either and exploded from the watery depths with a bilious croak. Clarice yelled in shock, Nolan uttered a very impolite word, and chaos erupted as the slimy monster attacked.

Taking careful aim proved impossible. The thing took up too much space, and given its bloblike appearance, didn't present a proper bull's-eye. Exactly where was its heart, or head for that matter? Unable to discern either, Clarice fired her weapon only to see her missiles get sucked into the gelatinous mass. Of more concern, her shots didn't seem to injure it at all. Not a good sign.

With no other recourse, she dove at it with her knife, slashing at the flailing limbs, which seemed to sprout from all over its body.

"Argh!" hollered Nolan. "I've been slimed."

He sure had, she thought with grim mirth as she spared him only the briefest of glances. Green goo covered Nolan's impeccable self and he wasn't happy about it. Her moment of inattention cost her. A tentacle popped out of nowhere and wrapped around her waist. She sliced at it, sawing it off, only to have another take its place. Then another. They wrapped around her, pinning her arms to her sides, their cold, clammy touch not as worrisome as the fact they slowly squeezed the very breath from her. Was this how her life ended? Underground, hugged to death by a blob? How revolting.

A mighty roar split the air and she blinked as a big lion crowned by a poufy golden mane appeared in her line of sight. The doctor to the rescue. She watched in fascination as the muscled feline dove at the blob, shredding the jellylike body with its razor sharp claws. *My, what big teeth he has*, or so she noted as his pointed canines ripped gobs of fleshy goo. The tentacles around her loosened as the creature reacted. It dropped her as it tried to retreat. But Nolan proved relentless, grabbing the creature and yanking it further onto the cement floor where he proceeded to systematically dissect it until all that remained were oozing, twitching pieces.

Wide-eyed and silent, Clarice for once could say she was impressed. The lion wasn't. Shaking his paws, he tried to dislodge the residual goo, but the stuff clung to his fur. Realizing that, beast morphed into man in a fluid change she envied. Then coveted because despite being covered in slime, Nolan was quite the man. Muscled man. Very naked man. Very disgusted naked man.

"Oh, that was seriously gross," he exclaimed, spitting to the ground. "Oh, what I wouldn't give for a shower and a toothbrush right now."

"Would you settle for a towel?" shouted an amused voice from above their heads. Distracted by the action, neither of them had noticed the hatch overhead opening and the grinning face of Mason peering down. "But first, say cheese."

And that was when chaos number two erupted as Nolan, with an even mightier roar than before, leapt up the ladder bellowing, "Erase that picture, bear!"

"Over my dead body, doc." Laughter filled his reply.

With a shake of her head, Clarice went to corral her slimy doctor and give her report. She also made a mental note to check the FUC forums for the posted images the second agent on scene took of Nolan's bare white ass as he chased Mason around trying to get his hands on the camera.

She'd give FUC one thing, they certainly knew how to keep a girl on her toes and entertained.

Chapter Nine

Stinking of river water—not by choice, Mason having chucked him in the river to sluice the goop off him—Nolan was understandably irritable. He stank. The spare clothes he'd borrowed chafed. His hair hung wet, stringy, and smelly around his head. And worst of all, he'd failed to impress Clarice.

Didn't a heroic act like his deserve some kind of acknowledgement? A hey, good job? Maybe a thank you kiss? A quickie around the corner?

Nope. On the contrary, his avian partner ignored him as she gave her report to the agents who showed up to aid them. When she told of his lion tearing the blob to bits, she neglected to add any adjectives like golden magnificence, muscled wonder, or handsome, brave, and selfless.

All that gross work to save her feathery ass and she couldn't even say thank you. And what did he get out of it? A picture of him covered in slime, stark naked, eyes and hair wild, posted to the FUC message board. Sigh. He'd never live it down. At least the angle of the camera hid the size of his junk, so hopefully he wouldn't have to change his phone number again.

Disgruntled, he didn't say a word to his partner when she straddled the bike and they left the FUC extermination team in charge of the underground crime scene. They'd found no sign of the other mutants either above ground or below, but just in case, a FUC team was going to investigate the sewer tunnels before gassing them and sealing the entrance up.

At this point, Nolan didn't care. Given what he'd faced in the dark hole, even he could no longer deny that saving his former patients seemed a lost cause. The inhuman creature he'd fought couldn't be saved. Hell, he couldn't even tell what it was, not without some hardcore DNA testing. Even then, they might never know for sure.

Annoyed at Clarice, he didn't snuggle her back as they got on the bike. He ignored Mason's jibes about riding bitch. Screw them all. He closed his eyes and slept.

Or meant to. It seemed he'd no sooner shut his orbs than they sprang open as he slammed into Clarice's back.

"What the hell?"

"Sorry." Funny how she didn't sound contrite.

"Any reason why you tried to give me whiplash?"

"I—um—that is…" She hemmed and hawed, pricking his curiosity.

"Is there a problem?"

"No. Yes. I mean, I know I didn't say anything back there, but, well, thank you." Oh, how begrudging it emerged.

He'd never heard anything more beautiful. "My pleasure."

Her head swiveled and he found himself captured by her gaze. For once, she didn't appear disparaging or mocking. "No, it's not. I can tell you're not a happy kitty. I mean, your hair is a mess and you stink to holy heaven, but what you did back there, saving me from that *thing*..." Her lips curled into a mouse of distaste. "It was really cool of you. Gross, but brave. And well, thanks."

"No problem." As easily as that, his irritation evaporated. And even when she tried to kill them, taking corners at high speeds, zipping through cars, and giving the finger to a semi truck bearing down on them with a guy three times his size, he didn't lose his good humor. Heck, even the whiff of his own body and a glimpse of his strawlike hair, which made his stomach roil, couldn't kill his good mood, and he no longer felt a need to sleep.

Given the adventure earlier in the day, he should have felt tired and in definite need of a nap, however, to his surprise, he found himself quite energized. Could it have something to do with the adrenaline-fueled fight? Partly. It had been a while since he'd fought a battle where the possibility of him actually getting hurt existed. Could it have to do with the fact he'd had to chase Mason around for half an hour until he caught the darned bear and confiscated his camera, deleting the ignoble image of him standing altogether covered in the most disgusting of fluids? A little. But, truthfully, he thought it had more to do with the way Clarice now regarded him.

Before, she'd eyed him with disdain. Oh sure, he knew she found him attractive, he could smell it. Sure, he'd caught her admiring his physique. But, when he saw her in danger, the blob slowly suffocating her, he snapped. Or as she later called it, "went completely feline on its slimy green ass!" His lion, with no regard for his clothing, burst free and dove into the fray with a fury he'd never experienced. *Hear me fucking roar!*

It seemed when it came to Clarice's safety, nothing would stand in his way, not foul taste or icky slime, which clung stubbornly to his skin and hair. But the inconvenience? Totally worth the result. She no longer looked at him the same way. Dare he say she even threw him a look of admiration? Not a long one, mind you, but of enough duration, he caught it. In her eyes, he was no longer the useless, pain in her ASS or just an extremely handsome doctor. Now, he was the awesome, courageous, not-so-useless, extremely handsome doctor. A doctor who plotted naughty things for her ASS.

Right after he washed up. She insisted he go first, and he didn't argue, not with his hair in a state of horror no lion could tolerate. *Hair emergency!* He did offer to share the large shower, but she declined. A pity. The fun they could have had with hot water and some soap…

As he made us of the various cleansing lotions and solutions, he placated his disappointment with the knowledge that while her mouth said no, her body said yes. She might not realize it, but he could smell it every time he roused her interest. Scented the musk that made her a liar. Why she kept denying her attraction, he wanted to find out.

First, he tried a frontal assault. Wearing just a towel, he emerged from the bathroom, hair wet but shiny clean, upper torso bare and moist. He caught her off guard and she froze mid-sentence on the phone.

"I—uh—sorry, can you repeat that?" Clarice turned her back to him and he pursed his lips. How long could he stand there before his actions came across as intentional instead of casual? *This is my place. Who says I don't wander around in a towel all of the time?* With a feline prowl to his step, he entered her line of vision, but pretended to ignore her as he headed for the fridge. He also strained to hear who she spoke to.

"Things are fine. I'm currently staying with a team member who requires a protective detail."

What? He frowned at the shelves in his fridge. He'd proven himself capable of taking care of himself and her. Didn't he deserve the title of partner?

"I'm hoping to wrap things up within the next few days and come home."

So soon? For some reason, the idea didn't sit well at all. He slammed the jug of milk on the counter, slid over the cookie jar, and plopped down to chew on chocolate chip goodness while sipping the creamy brew. He also didn't even bother to hide the fact he watched her pacing, doing her best to ignore him.

"Listen. I've got to go. I'll call you back tomorrow." She hung up the phone.

"Who was it?" He might have asked a little more tersely than he'd meant because she arched a brow.

"Why do you care?"

He shrugged. "Who says I do?" Now who was the liar?

"Just reporting my current status back home."

"Boyfriend worried?" Surely he didn't sound jealous?

A smirk ghosted across her lips. "Is this your way of asking if I'm single? I wouldn't have thought a lion interested in one night stands only cared."

"I don't." He did.

"Good."

Away she strode toward the bathroom and he realized she'd not answered his query. Did she have someone waiting for her? Someone she cared about? *We can take care of any competition,* his inner feline growled. There was gravy in the cupboard perfect for poultry.

"Doesn't he have a problem with you staying with a single guy?" He caught her just before she shut the bathroom door.

She popped her head out. "I don't belong to any man, Sylvester." And with that, she slammed the door shut.

Single. Yes!

Not that a boyfriend would have stopped him. Nolan was much too intrigued by his falcon partner to let something like a lover get in his way. Sometime between the sewer fight and now, he'd made up his mind to go after the hot chick and ruffle her feathers. *That ASS is mine!*

Speaking of which, hers was currently naked in a hot shower. What better time to begin the seduction of his reluctant avian partner than when she was at her most vulnerable? And least armed.

Using a claw, he popped the lock on the bathroom door and entered. The shower curtain was pulled tight, the hot steam thick. He padded forward on silent, bare feet and almost reached the waterproof fabric hiding her from view when the sharp edge of a knife pressed against his jugular.

"Exactly what are you doing, Sylvester?"

He grinned. *That's my girl.* She might not possess his sense of smell, but she was sharp in other ways. He liked that about her. He paid her weapon no mind and turned to face her. "Just checking on you. You've been in here a long time and I worried that perhaps you'd caught something during our time in the sewer.

She eyed him with suspicion. "Caught what?"

"Who knows what kind of germs lurk down there."

She shuddered. "Don't remind me."

"As your doctor, I really should check you over," he cajoled, taking a risk and placing his hands on her waist over the towel she'd wrapped around her dripping torso.

"I'm fine."

"I'm the doctor, so I think I should be the judge of that."

"You do?" Her lip curled a bit at the edge and the hand holding the knife dropped to her side. "And what tests did you plan to run?"

"Well, I really should do an all-over-body one, look for lesions where infection could possibly take root."

"I don't have any open wounds."

"Palpate you for sore spots that might indicate internal injury?"

"None of those either."

"Are you sure?" he asked as he pulled her against his body. He wound his arms around her in a hug. "How does this feel?"

"Fine," she replied. "No pain at all."

Perhaps not, but her heart rate did quicken, her pupils dilated, and her temperature inched up a notch. "Mind saying *ah* so I can take a peek in your mouth?"

"This really isn't necessary. There's nothing wrong with—"

Ah, screw the pretense. Tired of her fighting the inevitable, Nolan leaned in and took her mouth with his, silencing her.

Mmmm. Arousal instantly ignited, a smoldering fire he only felt when he touched her.

"I think," he said in between nibbles, "that you're running a bit of a fever."

"It is a touch hot in here," she mumbled back before sucking his lower lip.

"Let me fix that." He yanked. Off came her towel, leaving her gloriously naked for his roaming hands. To his gratification, she moaned and arched against him, her arms rising to twine around his neck, stretching her glorious lean length against his. They kissed as if they would starve without each other. Their tongues twined and knotted, danced and weaved, their breaths mixing, short and hot pants. Only one thing marred the moment. The damned towel around his waist. He broke off the kiss as he leaned back against the vanity. Spreading his thighs, his sarong style covering dropped to the floor. The revelation of his groin drew her gaze and her eyes widened. Indecision showed up in the form of her biting her lower lip.

Oh no. He was not letting her change her mind. He needed her. They need this. He tugged her into the vee his legs formed, cradling her, capturing her passion swollen lips to resume the embrace. Cupping her taut buttocks, he squeezed them. How could he have thought her too lean? The round, toned globes were a perfect fit for his palms.

It wasn't the only perfect thing about her. He left the hot pleasure of her mouth to trail hot kisses down the silky column of her neck, nibbling his way to the high, pert breasts he'd dreamed of. Her nipples, small perfect berries, awaited his consumption, and consume them he did, lavishing each with attention, his lips tugging and sucking at them as she pulled his hair, each gasp from her lips a ghostly caress to his ever growing desire.

And desire her he did. Never before had he so wanted to sink into a woman. To put his mark on a female and possess her. It was that fact, that possessive urge he knew would frighten his flighty bird, that held him back. Clarice would fly if pushed too fast. So he did something that no woman ever got from him before. He gave with no expectation of receiving.

Down to his knees he dropped, his hands holding her steady as his mouth found the bare mound she'd once boasted of. He held her quivering frame as his tongue delved between her soft folds and stroked her clit. He lapped at her, savoring her cream, absorbing her flavor, inhaling her rich aroma. More decadent than anything he'd ever encountered, Nolan pleasured his sweet

Clarice, bringing her to the brink of climax, then retreating, prolonging the erotic moment.

She tasted so sweet. He could have licked her all day. Her clit swelled under his attention. Her hips thrust against his mouth. Her fingers tangled in his hair, pulling and digging into his scalp, begging him without saying a word. Unless her *Ohs* of pleasure counted.

Over and over he teased her heavenly pussy, thrusting his tongue into her pulsing sex and moaning as she squeezed it with her muscles. He returned to her clit, his raspy tongue rubbing over the sensitized nub until her breathing came in erratic and short, mewling pants. So close. Almost there. He could feel her orgasm within reach. He grazed her swollen nub with his teeth. Once. Twice. A third time…

She came apart. And it was glorious.

Roaring in his head with victory, he held her up as she cried out and thrashed, the pleasure taking her on a wild ride, a ride he prolonged with caresses. Usually, this was where he'd bend her over and take his own turn. But this was Clarice.

So despite the fact she panted, "More. Give me more. Give me your cock," he held back. He wanted her to remember this moment. This pleasure. This gift for her and her alone.

He brought one hand into play and thrust two fingers into her velvety moistness while his tongue kept laving, the roughness of it even in his human form a gentle friction against her nub. Hot damn, did she like that. Gone was the in control agent. Vanished was the woman others perceived as cold and uptight. In her place writhed a seductress, one filled with fire and passion.

"Enough. Oh God. Not again. Don't stop. Oh God." She cried out and bucked against his sensual torture. Thrashed and thrust. He held her firm and didn't let up, his tongue flicking quickly across her clit, his fingers pumping in and out of her pulsing sex. The clench of her pussy when her climax hit just about crushed his fingers.

"Oh yes. Nolan!" She screamed *his* name as her second orgasm hit her even harder than the first and this time, he couldn't help a roar of satisfaction.

She is mine! Whether she accepted it yet or not, he staked his claim. She might fight and deny him, for the moment, but he would stalk her, fight for her, because Clarice was *the one.*

With one last long lick, he pulled himself reluctantly to his feet and drew her shivering frame to his chest. He hugged her as she recovered, content to bask in her diminishing glow despite his own need.

Having gotten to know her somewhat, he expected the shove that sent him reeling back. The hard poke to his ribs was uncalled for, though.

"You shouldn't have done that."

"You needed it."

She frowned. "Bad kitty."

"That's not what you screamed a minute ago."

"I faked it," she lied.

He quirked an eyebrow.

She turned red. "Okay, I didn't. But it can't happen again. And no one can ever know. I'd never live it down."

"I am not the type to brag."

"Then why do you look like the cat who ate the canary?"

"I look nothing at all like Grandpa Joe, thank you very much."

She didn't have a reply for that.

"So, are you coming?" he asked as he left her to enter his room and get dressed.

Again, silence.

He peered over his shoulder and saw her still standing where he left her, confusion on her face. "Well?"

"I am not sleeping with you."

He grinned. "I didn't mean that kind of coming. Although, I could be persuaded. What I actually meant was, are you coming with me to my aunt's for dinner?"

"Dinner?"

"Yes. You know that thing people do when they're hungry. Eat. Food. Filling your tummy." He patted his trim stomach and watched her gaze drop. He'd not yet managed to quell the swelling of his cock, and she noticed. Oh how she noticed. Standing out straight from his body, his cock stood at attention, just begging her to do something.

For a moment, he thought he might get some action. Her nipples hardened. She licked her lips and damn him if he couldn't smell her arousal surging again. The twitch of his dick broke the spell. Up flew her gaze.

"I don't think going out is a good idea given what's going on."

"Oh, they won't care we're having sex."

"We are not having sex."

"Sorry. I should have said they won't care if I've already eaten so long as I show up."

"Would you stop with the innuendos?" Clarice was practically cross-eyed at his deliberate twisting of her words. He hid a grin. "I meant going anywhere with the psychos still on the loose is a bad idea."

"No, missing the monthly dinner at my aunt's is not a good idea, given her temper. When she gets riled, my cousins get antsy. Ever been ambushed by a bunch of yowling cats? Not pretty, I can assure you." As family functions went, there were a few things he couldn't skip. Funerals, the monthly Sunday brunch, weddings, birthdays, and dinner at his aunt's. To do so resulted in horrifying consequences. Just ask his friend Harold from the next pride over. He'd decided to stay home and nurse a cold on his sister's birthday. He woke up the next morning, his mane shaved, and every part of his body smooth and hairless. His stubbly head was a grim reminder not to ever mess with the women of the pride, not where cake and presents were concerned.

"Let me get this straight, you want me, a bird, to knowingly attend a dinner hosted by—how many large felines?"

"Oh, probably about a dozen or more, give or take, depending on who's back from where. I've a got a few cousins serving our country overseas. My mother found it best to keep as many of them as busy as possible given the shortage of male lions to entertain them."

"I think I should pass."

"I figured you might. Can't say as I blame you what with my mother going and all."

Clarice froze in the process of grabbing her towel from the floor. "Wait. Did you say your mother is going to be there?"

"Yes. So it's probably best you not go. You can drop me off and pick me up later. I won't tell Kloe."

"On second thought, I do have orders to not let you out of my sight."

"I'll be surrounded by a dozen or more lionesses. I think you can rest assured of my safety."

"Still, though, I wouldn't want to be negligent in my duties."

Why oh why did he not trust the evil smile that crossed her lips? Why oh why did it make her look so deliciously sexy? And why did his sick sense of humor look forward to the dinner now that he knew Clarice was coming? *Because one thing is for sure, it won't be boring.*

Chapter Ten

What the hell am I doing?

Clarice wondered, not for the first time since meeting the lion, if she needed to check her sanity. *Exactly what prompted me to volunteer to accompany Nolan to a dinner with way too many felines?* She could have just driven him to his aunt's house and dropped him off. She could have sat in his posh car, listened to some tunes, caught up on the news, and watched the house from the street. The probability of him coming to harm was practically nonexistent because even the mutants they hunted wouldn't dare accost him with that many large predators around. Yet, there she stood at his side on the front step even though she knew his mother and her gaggle of kitties wouldn't welcome her. So why did she do it?

Curiosity for one, which killed the cat, but did what to the bird? Then there was her insane urge to needle Nolan's mother. Nothing out of the ordinary there, more inexplicable was the part of her, which for some morbid, unknown reason wanted to see Nolan in a family setting.

What kind of nephew and cousin was he? What did a family of cats resemble when they got together? She just had to find out for herself despite the possibility of ending up as dinner.

In the orphanage, mealtime was a noisy affair with the fledglings yattering and fighting over food. Fistfights often erupted, as did sudden showers of feathers as the wild hatchlings lost control and got involved in aerial fights. Would the same thing happen here?

Should she have brought a lint brush and a hairball remedy just in case? Strangely enough, she didn't fear for her safety despite walking into a feline pride. Sure, she knew she couldn't take on that many cats at once, but she thought she knew Nolan well enough by now, especially since the incident in the sewer, to guess he wouldn't let her come to harm, even from his family. Obsessed with his hair or not, her doctor possessed a chivalrous side and more courage than his foppish exterior would indicate. He'd keep his family from eating her. *But will that prevent him from eating me?*

She hoped not. Despite her earlier protestation, she had quite enjoyed his oral assault on her female parts. Very much enjoyed, enough she wouldn't mind him doing it again. Maybe she would even reciprocate. Not that she'd admit to any such thing aloud. Hopefully, he'd come to that conclusion on his own—if not, she could always give him a push and accidentally fall on top of him.

However, now was not the time to think about his deft tongue, agile fingers, and the body part she'd yet to test-drive—but had seen. Damn did he have a lot to brag about. No wonder the ladies chased him. It still amazed her that despite his obvious need, he'd pleasured her with no expectation of anything in return.

What man did that?

Nolan apparently. The jerk kept doing the unexpected and throwing her off balance. Worse, she found herself liking him more and more. A lot more. *I hope it's not obvious.* Judging by the sly glance he slid her and the half-smile curling her lips, the jerk might have guessed. She adopted a stony expression, trying to not give any of her erotic thoughts. She apparently failed. So when he snickered? She elbowed him in the ribs. The blow didn't even cause him to gasp, although he did chuckle and murmur, "Save that energy for later."

The door swung open and a short, gap-toothed youngster grinned at them. "Uncle Nolan!"

"Hey, trouble," he replied, swinging the girl up in one arm and giving her a hug. He stepped over the threshold and Clarice debated for one last moment if she should follow. *Chicken.* She didn't need to hear her internal cluck to decide. She paused at the threshold of his aunt's home on the outskirts of town, a sprawling ranch style that boasted many tall trees, perfect for nesting, as the babble of voices washed over her. *Can I do this?*

Setting his niece down, Nolan peered back at her and whispered, "Are you sure you want to do this? It's not too late to back out."

Cluck. Cluck. "I'm not afraid." Spine straight, eschewing the hand he tried to lock around her fingers, she strode ahead of him, moving from the vestibule into domestic chaos. Women of all shapes and ages lounged around, not all of them in human form. On the floor, a pair of cubs tumbled in a spitting mass of golden fur, while atop a wide, and hopefully bolted, entertainment unit, a lean lioness napped. It took only a second for all talk to cease. Way too many eyes turned her way, assessing the stranger in their midst. Clarice wondered how many of them pictured her breaded and deep-fried. She already knew of one feline who thought she was finger-licking good. She bit her lip lest she giggle aloud.

"Nolan," purred a golden-haired beauty wearing only the skimpiest of shorts and a top. "You brought fresh meat. How sweet."

"She's my guest, Yanna, so claws off."

The blonde named Yanna pouted, but his comment didn't deter the others from surging toward them, veiled insults and threats flying.

"Smells like chicken."

"Kind of scrawny, if you ask me."

"I thought we were having lasagna for dinner?"

"Hey, who didn't change the toilet paper roll when they were done?"

Surrounded by predators, Clarice stood her ground, even if every instinct in her screamed to fly away before one of the cats pounced.

"Would this be the right or wrong time to quote Looney Tunes?" she muttered to Nolan. He hid a choked laugh behind a fist and she inwardly smiled. She could handle a little ribbing so long as they didn't attempt to do any plucking.

"Nolan, about time you showed up," hollered a familiar voice. Yay, his mother was already here. "I see you brought the giant ASS."

"Aunt Brenda! Mind your mouth around the children." One of the female's present took offense while a petite brunette rolled her eyes.

"Oh please. Like they haven't heard worse."

Entering the room, Brenda appeared more relaxed than during their morning encounter, probably because Clarice now entered her turf. "Cool it, Nessa. Jo-Jo's right. They've heard worse than that. And besides, that's what she is. An ASS." Brenda relished saying it way too much. Clarice held her tongue. "Family, say hello to Clarice Tertius. She's from Avian Soaring Security and is here on loan to FUC."

Nolan didn't even bother holding back his grin as a chorused "Oh" echoed through the room.

"What does FUC need ASS for?" asked a new voice.

"Aren't you old enough to know the answer to that?" said another female with a snicker.

"Get your mind out of the gutter," yipped a third.

And from there, Clarice seemed more or less forgotten as the women went back to bickering and in general just making noise.

Nolan visibly relaxed. "Well, that went better than expected."

"It did?" Cheeks hot with embarrassment, Clarice crossed her arms.

"I'd say it did. They didn't strip you naked, force you to change, and tar you like they did the chicken hawk last year. But in their defense, he deserved it."

"What did he do?"

"Asked Abigail to dance at a club."

"And that was grounds for a taffy?" A taffy, known in the avian world as a tar and feather.

"Nah, it was the fact he used Abigail to make his girlfriend jealous that got him in trouble."

"I'd have to agree then he deserved it."

"How do you punish wingless ones who do you wrong?"

"Honeyed and rolled in birdseed or bread crumbs."

"That doesn't sound as bad."

"Then we drop them on a beach and let the seagulls say hello."

Nolan let out a huge belly laugh. "Remind me to never piss you off in front of your friends then."

What made him think he'd ever meet them?

"What's so funny?" his mother asked, butting in.

"Just discussing cultural differences," Nolan replied with a wink in her direction.

"Has your aunt met Clarice yet? Of course, she hasn't. Let me rectify that."

Clarice didn't have much of a choice as the matriarch grabbed her by the hand and dragged her through the bodies, which magically parted to let her pass. She peeked over her shoulder and saw Nolan shrug helplessly and mouth, "Good luck."

Not exactly reassuring, and neither was the gigantic pot on the most massive stove she'd ever seen. Birds were, by and large, picky eaters. Most tended toward the slim side given every extra pound made flight that much more strenuous. It seemed cats didn't feel the same way. Or at least not the feline in charge of the enormous kitchen. Brandishing a wooden spoon covered in a red sauce, she barked out orders to her minions who scurried this way and that, stirring, seasoning, and in general creating a medley of smells. Clarice salivated and could have sworn she gained weight just from the thought of ingesting the rich foods currently cooking.

"Why do I smell chicken?" yelled the woman in charge. "Who brought poultry in here? You know how my Alfred feels about white meat."

"Probably the same way I feel," muttered Clarice. "Although, I do like fish."

What scent didn't achieve, a few lowly spoken words did. The attention of the chef veered her way and dark brows shot high. "What the hell did you bring into my house, Brenda?"

"I didn't bring her. Nolan did." Smug didn't even start to describe the naughty grin on the matriarch's face.

"Nolan's dating a turkey?"

How rude. "I'm a falcon, thank you very much, and no, we are not dating." *Just indulging in oral sex.*

"It's an ASS/FUC thing," Brenda said with a negligent wave of her hand. To their credit, only one sous chef snickered at the mix of the acronyms. Clarice herself had to bite her tongue. Really, who came up with these names? Had to be a man with a perverted sense of humor. "Clarice, meet my sister, Shirley."

"Nice to meet you, ma'am."

"Don't ma'am me. I'm not old like my sister here. Call me Shirley."

"Old? Who are you calling old?" Brenda bristled.

Shirley ignored her and brandished her spoon. "You've got a lot of balls to willingly come to a house full of cats, especially before I've fed them their dinner, turkey girl."

"Falcon."

"Whatever. You all smell the same once you're stuffed and cooked."

That was so not reassuring. But Clarice wouldn't let something like feeling at a disadvantage curb her acerbic wit. "Well, I've always wanted to see the inside of a cathouse, although, I've got to say, I expected more red velour and scratching posts."

It took them a second to get the jibe, then Shirley let out a guffaw. "Great big balls indeed. I like her."

"She's got guts for a skinny bird," whispered someone in the back.

"Too stringy to eat," grumbled another.

"You say Nolan brought her?" Shirley eyed her up and down and shared a look with Brenda, who shrugged.

Suspicious, Clarice asked, "Yeah, he brought me. Why are you both acting like it's such a big deal? He said he couldn't miss dinner. I'm supposed to keep watch over him so I came. End of story."

"He said he couldn't miss it?" His mother snickered. "Technically, he's right, but he usually only pops in for dessert. Grabs a piece of pie and runs. He rarely makes the meal part."

Oh, really?

"And he's never brought a girl before," added the aunt.

"He never brings girls anywhere there's family," piped up one of the cousins.

"You'd almost think we embarrass him."

"You mean we don't?"

Ignoring the joking, Clarice's lips nearly disappeared into her face she tightened them so straight. "Excuse me. I need to have a word with Sylvester."

"Sylvester? Who's Sylvester? I thought she came with Nolan?" Shirley asked in a whisper that carried.

"Hush. I want to hear this."

Back out to the front room Clarice marched and halted. The anger coursing through her at the way Nolan had manipulated her into coming, for reasons she'd yet to discern, evaporated. In its place, warmth spread. She tried to fight it. Tried to regain her indignation, but couldn't, not when faced with the cute scene presenting itself in the form of one large male sprawled on the floor letting a gaggle of cubs use him as a toy.

Gentle, yet with obvious enjoyment, the damned lion played with the children, ruffling their fur, letting them gnaw on him, playing slap paw. He even—gasp—let them mess up his usually tidy hair and impeccable tie. Then the jerk had the nerve amidst all the cuteness to catch her eye and give her the slowest, sexiest grin in all existence. How dare he?

"Uh-oh, I think Nolan's in trouble," someone muttered.

Damn straight he was. Clarice growled and whirled on her toes, stalking to the front door. He caught up to her outside.

"Hey, where are you going? We haven't eaten yet. Did you get a call from the office?"

"Yeah, actually, I did. My rational self called and said to get away from the big, lying pussycat."

"What did I lie about?"

Deny it, would he? Ha. Like hell. "You brought me here on purpose." She poked him in the chest.

"No, you volunteered to come."

"But as it turns out, we didn't have to stay," she accused.

"Nope."

What? He wasn't even going to try and lie his way out of it. "You didn't mention that part."

"You didn't ask. All I said was I needed to make an appearance."

"Which implies staying for a while."

"Implies, but I never said it. You assumed, hence, I didn't lie."

"Don't you dare split hairs."

"Never. My conditioner is too good for that." She glared at his paltry attempt at humor. He grinned. "Would you rather I split feathers?"

She punched him in the gut, ignoring the low "Ooh" from the crowd watching in the open doorway.

"We really need to work on your communication skills," he gasped.

"Why? I think I just communicated my annoyance with you quite efficiently."

"True. But you could have just said, 'I'm mad.'"

She growled.

A smile curled his lips, a boyish one she fought to not melt under. “Have I told you how sexy it is when you make that sound?”

No, and she wouldn’t let it distract her. “Why did you goad me into coming?”

He shrugged. “You told me you didn’t have any family growing up. I thought you might enjoy a taste of mine.”

“Why would I enjoy it? They’re cats. I’m a bird.”

“Lions, if you please, who immediately accepted you.”

“How do you figure that?”

“Well, you’re standing here talking to me, aren’t you, instead of boiling in a pot with some carrots and celery?”

“You have a sick sense of humor, Sylvester.”

“Like you don’t.”

She didn’t reply, because honestly, she kind of enjoyed his jabs. Even those of his mother and cousins. How deranged did that make her?

“Come on back inside. We’ll eat some lasagna. Gorge ourselves on bread and then pig out on the best cherry pie ever.”

“Thanks, Nollie!” yelled Aunt Shirley.

“Nollie?” She snickered.

“Don’t you dare repeat it,” he warned, but his eyes twinkled with mirth.

“Only if you tell me why your uncle Alfred hates poultry.”

"Oh, he doesn't hate it, but his best friend is an ostrich. Out of respect to him, my aunt doesn't cook any aerial critters except for turkey at Christmas and Thanksgiving. But don't worry, she only buys from certified dealers. No sentient birds are ever used in the making of any dish in her house."

"Does this mean I should keep my love of authentic Chinese food secret from your family?"

Nolan bit his lip as several voices gasped. "You are truly evil."

"You're just figuring that out now?"

For a moment, she thought he'd kiss her. The expression in his eyes certainly seemed to indicate he would. And despite their avid audience, by damn, she was going to let him.

Or would have if one of his damned cousins hadn't ruined the moment with a shouted, "Dinner you love birds! Last one to the table is a rotten egg."

To everyone's laughter, Nolan earned the title, but he didn't seem to care as he lounged amidst the pride of females and one aging uncle. Even stranger, Clarice felt right at home among them. And he was right about one thing. His aunt made the best damned cherry pie ever.

Chapter Eleven

Stay or go. Stay or go.

Lester mulled his choices as he laid the doctor's home to waste. It offended him that while he spent all those months locked up in a cell, the undeserving doctor got to live like a king. So unfair. Just because lions were big and strong, and fast with big teeth—and great hair—didn't mean they deserved the title king of the jungle.

Everyone knew chimps were smarter. Much smarter. Hadn't he shown it by locating the doctor's home, which that stupid nurse so conveniently left for him to find in her address book? Getting in proved so easy. All he had to do was follow a couple leaving the place. A simple bump of the lady, a swipe of her wallet, and presto, he got her key card. Slipping into the parking garage took only moments as he scuttled in on the bumper of a car before slipping off into the shadows. Avoiding the cameras in the elevator, he took the stairs, hugging the walls and jumping from floor to floor using the railing, keeping him out of sight until he reached the doctor's floor.

He spent a moment cursing and stomping his feet in the hall when he realized his key card wouldn't open the doctor's condo. But that was when he discovered an interesting side effect of the mastermind's experimentation. He could move things. With his mind!

Just another sign of his greatness. All it took was him staring at the lock for a moment as his anger built before, with a loud click, the tumbler he imagined turned, giving him access.

Once inside, he meant to wait for the doctor. Catch the golden-haired feline by surprise. Lion or not, one good swing of a metal bar would knock him out. But, a prowl of the doctor's quarters revealed a second scent. An unknown had spent the night on the couch. A guard most likely. It sent Lester into a rage.

One target he could handle, but two? It wasn't fair. He needed his revenge. Needed blood. Needed popcorn, which the doctor thankfully had in the form of microwavable bags located in a cupboard. *Crunch. Crunch. Crunch.*

Once he calmed down—three bags of popcorn later—he realized staying to confront at least two predators, even if one was a bird, might not be in his best interest, new super power or not.

Lucky for him, he came up with a new plan. He just needed patience to implement it. Patience and more popcorn to tide him over. Lots of popcorn, and he knew just the place to get it.

Chapter Twelve

Speculation abounded amongst his family members. None of them ever came right out and asked him why he'd brought Clarice, but he saw the question in their eyes. *And what would I have replied if they did ask?*

He could have stuck to the cover story of Clarice acting as a layer of protection against some crazy shifters, but the real truth? Much more complex. How could he explain that she fascinated him? Not in a scientific or medical way, but in a when-a-man-met-a-woman, *the woman*, fashion, and felt an instant connection. How could he reveal that unlike all the felines and other women who'd thrown themselves at him, Clarice was the one who wouldn't leave his mind? Wouldn't leave his thoughts? The one he dreamed about when he closed his eyes. The one he sought when he opened them. How frightened he'd felt when he saw her facing death. The one who roused his protective instinct. How could he admit just how exquisite she'd appeared and tasted when she let herself go and indulged in passion? *Let herself go with me, something I wager she doesn't do often.* That in and of itself awed him. Made him feel special. Made him feel…needed.

Needed for more than his position, money, his great hair, or ability to sire lions.

How do I tell my family, my mother, my pride, that I think I'm falling in love with a falcon? They'd castrate him for sure. Lecture him about cross breeding. Lock him in a room and threaten him with hair removal. Or would they?

It seemed he wasn't the only one won over by his tough chick. Despite the ribbing and sly threats, Clarice gave as good as she got, and in return, his family seemed to have accepted her. At least on the surface. What their reaction would be if they thought his relationship with Clarice extended beyond that of coworker or lover remained to be seen. But, for now, they seemed willing to accept her within their fold.

However, that could all change in a moment. If his mother thought for one minute Nolan would settle down with a falcon of all things instead of a sanctioned feline, he had no doubt things would get hairy.

For now, he'd just have to keep the burgeoning thing growing between them under wraps. And not just from his mother. He suspected if Clarice caught even an inkling that his feelings for her extended beyond flirtation or work, she'd take flight. She'd made it clear what she thought of him. Desire was one thing. Expecting her to willingly enter into a relationship with him? A whole different ballgame.

"Are we going back to your place or do we have to visit more family members?" she asked as they left his aunt's house amidst a chorus of goodbyes and not so discreet suggestions of what they should do for the rest of the evening. Some of them not far from his own ideas on the matter.

"What do you say we go home? We've done our duty and now have the rest of the evening free." Free to do whatever they pleased. Hopefully, without any clothing.

To his surprise, she didn't argue. "Sounds good. I'm driving." As if he didn't already guess that, given she'd kept the keys and she slid in the driver seat.

Getting in on the other side, the sweet perfume of her arousal surrounded him, a musk he couldn't escape in the close confines of the car. What brought it on, he didn't know. He sure hoped it wasn't because he let her drive again. He preferred to think he was the cause of her excitement and not some hunk of metal. How strange to feel jealous of his car. Testing the waters, he casually slid his hand onto her thigh as he engaged her in conversation.

"How did you enjoy dinner?"

"It was interesting."

"Interesting how?"

She shrugged. "Your family bickers a lot, and yet, you can feel the affection they have for each other."

"We might fight and call each other names, but we do have each other's backs. What about you? There must be someone in your life, a best friend, aunt, uncle…" He already knew the boyfriend answer.

She shook her head. "My family was never large to begin with. My mother was an only child and my grandparents died before my birth."

"You never say anything about your father."

He could almost smell her embarrassment. "Because my mother didn't know who he was. I was conceived during a one night stand at some bar out west. All she remembered was he was human with long lashes. Not exactly much to go on."

"So you lucked out getting the full shifter gene?"

A roll of her shoulders accompanied her reply. "I guess. But sometimes I have to wonder if I'd have been better off human. At least then I might have fit in somewhere. Once my mom died and I entered the orphanage aerie, I was alone. Most of the kids were there only part-time. Stopovers, as I called them. Most of them had extended family who could take them in. I, on the other hand, ended up a lifer. It kind of set me apart."

He ached for her. His poor Clarice. He couldn't imagine a life without someone at his back, or on his side. No wonder she adopted a tough persona. No wonder she didn't let people get close. "Let me guess, these so-called stopovers weren't exactly kind about your situation."

"They were kids. Kids are cruel. Besides, they were right. I was the girl no one wanted."

He heard the unspoken—*that no one loved.* "But it wasn't your fault."

"Maybe. Maybe not. I wasn't exactly the cuddliest child. I got into fights. Bloodied a few beaks. Plucked a few feathers. No one wants a little girl who can brawl like a full grown rooster." The loneliness and pain she fought to hide with her flippant tone made him bristle.

"A pride would have. We value strength."

"But I'm not a feline. And we of the avian persuasion do things differently."

"I don't like it."

"No one said you had to."

Needing to change the subject before he went furry and hunted down each and every child who made her feel bad, he asked, "So how did you end up an ASS?"

"There's not many options for someone without money, family, or connections. Joining the Avian Soaring Security group gave me a chance for education and a future."

And a sense of belonging, he'd wager. "Do you like it?"

Again, she shrugged. "Most of the time. I'm good at what I do; however, there are politics involved, as I'm sure you've seen in FUC."

Speaking of politics, some things he'd read when doing his background search on his new partner made more sense. "In other words, as a woman without a family, you deal with idiots who think they can take advantage of you and get away with it."

She tossed him a sharp look. "What makes you say that?"

"Oh please. Give me some credit. Just like you looked into me, I happened to have a peek at your file."

"And?"

"You passed your courses with flying colors. Graduated top of your class. You've got an exemplary record when it comes to hunting down criminals. You should be ranked higher than you are."

"No kidding." She couldn't hide her grudging tone.

"Yet you're not because you obviously pissed off the wrong guy. So who did you turn down for sex?"

"Who says I did?"

"Because the guy who ordered you to work with FUC is the father of the male who filed charges against you for assaulting him."

A smirk pulled up one corner of her mouth. "Nice detective work, Sylvester."

"I'm not just pretty, you know."

"So I'm starting to see. And you're mostly right."

"Ack!" He grabbed his chest. "I think I'm dying. She finally admits it."

"Stop it before I stop this car and kill you for real."

"Oh please, we both know you won't kill me. Hurt me, maybe, but kill? Nah."

"What makes you so certain?"

"Because then you wouldn't be able to enjoy what I have planned for you when we get back to my place."

"And just what do you have planned, Sylvester? I already told you I wasn't getting involved. What happened after my shower was a one-time thing. You caught me during a moment of weakness."

"Really?" He let his hand slide up her thigh, a hand, he might add, she'd never bothered to move since he placed it there. Her breathing hitched. "I think," he purred, "that you're protesting out of habit."

"You do?"

"Yes. I think you want me to touch you." He palmed her sex and the car jerked, but her focus never wavered from the road before them. The fact she would not let her gaze stray told him as much as the rising scent of her arousal. He'd expected her to stubbornly fight, though. All part of her charm. "I think you want me just as much as I want you."

"I think you're conceited."

"I am. But you're wet. For me. For this." He rubbed her and she couldn't halt the soft moan that slipped from her lips.

"I'm supposed to be keeping an eye on you."

"What better way than if we're skin to skin?"

"I need to stay on my guard for danger."

"Oh trust me, my lion won't let anything sneak up on us." And if anything tried, and interrupted, he'd probably rip them to shreds.

"We're too different."

"You know what they say, opposites attract."

"I don't want a relationship."

"Who says we're having one? Nothing wrong with some good old-fashioned sex. No strings. Just pleasure. Hot. Trembling. Skin-to-skin. Pleasure." He leaned into her as he whispered the last few words, his breath feathering her skin.

She shivered and again the car wobbled. "You're going to get us killed," she rasped.

"I'll behave. For now. But do you mind getting us back to the condo a little quicker? I can only wait for so long."

Their speed, which had dipped as he teased her, shot up as she floored the gas. He might have laughed at the sign of her eagerness, but he held it in. He didn't want anything to change her mind. They made it to the parking garage without incident and in silence, the sexual tension between them strung tight. As soon as they disembarked from his car, they took quick steps to the elevator. Even before the doors slid shut, he closed in on her, his mouth seeking hers, hungry for a taste. She met him in a clash of teeth and tongue, her arousal just as fervent.

By all that was holy, she set him on fire. He couldn't get enough, from her sweet cherry pie taste to her hot breath panting. She roused the carnal beast in him, the savage, the animal who wanted more than to just sink his cock inside. He wanted to bite her and leave a mark for everyone to see. He wanted to roar to the world to stay away from her because she belonged to him. He wanted her, needed her. But did she need and want him back?

The sensual slide of her tongue over his and the frantic thrust of her pelvis against his cock seemed to say yes. But lust ruled her right now. Ruled them both. Answers to his questions would have to wait. He dared not do anything to break their sensual, passionate spell.

All too soon, they arrived at his floor, the jarring ding of the bell and doors opening forcing them apart.

"We've arrived," she said breathlessly, her gaze locked on his.

"First one through the door gets to come first?"

"And if it's a tie?"

Oh, damn. His dick twitched at the thought of exploding inside her just as she climaxed. How wicked would that feel to have her flesh milking him as he came?

He growled in reply, the man succumbing to the passion of his beast, primal passion overtaking his manners as he swung her into his arms and strode down the hall. Halfway to his apartment, he smelled it, and he almost roared in frustration as he suddenly realized his evening would not end on the high note he hoped for. She didn't immediately notice his inattention, busy nibbling on the column of his neck. She even sucked at his skin hard enough to maybe leave a red mark, a stamp of ownership whether she intended it or not.

Distraction or not, body on fire or not, he couldn't succumb to the allure of her actions, not when his lion roused itself, its protective instincts kicking in. *Danger.* Yes, danger awaited in his apartment; he could smell it, feel it, sense it. It stroked his ego to realize he'd so unbalanced her that he noted it first. He tilted her chin and brushed her lips with a softly murmured, "We might have company."

Instantly, she stopped her nibbling caresses, the languorous sensuality she'd just exhibited replaced by the steel-edged version she showed the rest of the world. "Foe, I take it?"

He nodded as he set her on her feet.

"Dammit." Out came her gun and he saw her take deep, heaving breaths, steadying her racing pulse. He stored his pride in the fact he'd flustered her so deeply for later. Right now, they needed their wits about them.

Despite knowing she wouldn't stand for it, he tried to tuck her behind him—*I am after all the lion in this relationship, and it's my duty to protect her*—but like the females in the pride, she ignored him and took a position at his side, acting as his equal. He appreciated that. Unlike his female relatives, she didn't think him completely useless when it came to battle.

The door to his place gaped open an inch, even though he knew for a fact he'd completely latched it when they left earlier. Clarice pointed her gun hand at chest height and using the toe of her shoe, swung the portal wider. Nolan, tie loosened and shoes kicked off, readied himself to go furry.

Nothing jumped out at them, but the smell of wrongness grew stronger, the same scent he'd encountered at Agnes'. One of the missing psychos had found them.

In went Clarice, revolver pointed, Nolan at her heels, sniffing. He knew this scent. Recognized it. How could he not when he'd treated the male it belonged to, a male who hated doctors and blamed them all, even Nolan, for his torture at the hands of Mastermind? Unlike his nurse's home, there was no barbecue sauce or other people on the scene before him to muddy it.

"I know who it is," he whispered.

Clarice held a finger up to her lips.

"No need for silence. He's gone."

"How can you be sure?" she hissed.

"It's a jungle thing. I just know." His apartment *felt* empty. He couldn't really explain it any clearer than that. But while the intruder had departed, he'd certainly left his mark. Nothing remained intact. From his beautiful buttery soft leather sofas slashed to ribbons to his pristine carpet, stained beyond repair. The urine all over his bed, though, really beat all. It took a lot of willpower not to whip his dick out and spray over top of it. His lion seemed really insistent on making him cover up with his own mark.

Clarice, even with her feeble sense of smell, caught the acrid stench. "I guess you'll need a new mattress."

"New everything," he replied with a sigh. "Damn it. I guess I won't be taking that vacation to Mexico this year."

"Poor Sylvester."

"Don't start with me, woman."

She choked on a sound as she spun on a heel to peruse him. "Did you just call me *woman*?"

"I did. Now is not the time for your snide remarks. Not when my evening is ruined."

"Poor kitty cat. Did someone break his toys?" she sassed.

"No. Someone ruined what was promising to be the best sex of my life," he rumbled. Well, that certainly took her by surprise, or so he smugly wagered given her wide eyes, open mouth, and lack of retort. "You didn't seriously think I cared about this stuff? It's replaceable. What we almost indulged in, though…" He shook his head mournfully. "Delayed for who knows how long."

"Try forever."

"You wish, Tweety. You can stop denying it. I want you. You want me. The only question now is how long before we can get out of here, get checked into a hotel, and hop into a shower where I can worship you with my tongue and cock."

"Is that all you can think of? Sex?"

He blinked. "Well, yeah. Don't tell me you're not miffed we got interrupted?"

"I'd call this more than an interruption, Sylvester. One of the psychos was in your home."

"His name is Lester."

"Whatever. Doesn't the fact he entered your place bother you?"

"Sure. But there's no point in getting all dramatic about it." Okay, he lied. It did piss him off. Really pissed him off. And as for his lion? He held onto that beast by only the thinnest of leashes. Some jerk came into his home. *My home.* Invaded his space. Destroyed his things. Ruined his evening with a hot chick. However, dwelling on it wouldn't solve anything. Going off the deep end rarely did. So no matter how annoyed and violated he felt, Nolan would hold onto his temper and feelings, take care of the situation, get his woman to safety, make love to her—nap—make love to her again, then go hunt down the bastard who ruined his favorite cashmere freaking sweater.

"Wow. I'm impressed. If it had been me, I'd have flown the coop already looking to mete some vengeance."

"Oh, never fear, revenge is on the menu, but going off half-cocked won't solve anything."

"Now is the best time, though, while the trail is fresh."

"Not for long. We're not dealing with an idiot. Lester might be not in his right mind, but he's anything but stupid. He'll have covered his tracks. We need to outsmart him."

"So you weren't kidding? You recognized the scent."

"Yeah. I had an inkling at Agnes', but the contamination by the daughter and first responders muddied it. This time, though, there's no mistaking it. Lester pretty much ran around naked in this place." Which reminded him…he peered down at his bare feet. Damn. He'd need to scrub them, maybe dip them in some gasoline to disinfect.

"And Lester was which one?"

"Chimpanzee. Short fellow, about five-five, brown hair and eyes. Nurses thought he was cute, but he had a bad attitude."

"I remember his file. He was the one who argued the most with staff about staying under lock and key when we had him in custody."

"He really hated doctors and all things medical. I kind of felt bad for the guy. He was a fairly well-to-do fellow before Mastermind got her claws on him. Given his rage issues before the drug, I'd say he's got real issues now."

"You think?" She stared at his trashed condo pointedly. "So where do you suppose he went?"

Other than crazy? "How would I know? I still can't figure out how he got in." Building security wouldn't have let him waltz in. On the other hand, Lester had enough smarts to have obviously found a way. If he had to guess, he'd wager he came in through the underground, stole one of the elevator passes, and made his way up. But it still didn't explain how he managed to unlock his door.

"I've got to call this in." Clarice already had her phone out, dialing.

"Of course. I'll take a peek around and see if I spot anything odd." In the mess left behind, though, finding a clue would resemble the whole needle in a haystack trick. God, what a disaster. Even the kitchen was trashed. His microwave smoked, the smell of burnt popcorn making his nose twitch.

It didn't take long for him to realize everything needed to be tossed and burned. Lester left nothing intact. His rage seemed a boundless, violent thing, and that worried Nolan. If this was how his former patient reacted to his condo, how would he react if they met face to face? Not that Nolan feared for himself, a lion was a match for a chimp any day, even one hopped up on a drug, but what about Clarice? By associating with her, what kind of danger had he put her in? Especially since he could see Lester had gone through her bag and gotten her scent. Hell, he might have even caught the lingering perfume of their earlier lovemaking. Did Clarice now have a target on her back?

Forget her guarding him. Nolan needed to keep a close eye on *her*. He wouldn't let anyone, former patient or not, hurt his woman. He would, however, keep those thoughts to himself. Somehow, he doubted she would agree with his assessment that she needed protecting. Clarice believed herself invincible, but if the sewer taught him anything it was that while tough and competent with weapons, when it came down to a battle where brute force was involved, her slight weight and avian heritage put her at a disadvantage.

It seemed to take forever before a cleanup crew arrived, headed by his favorite bear, Mason. The agent whistled as he walked in. "Geez, doc. What the heck did you do to this guy to deserve this? Did you probe him rectally one too many times with latex gloves?"

"I tried to help him."

"I take it Lester didn't appreciate it."

"You think?"

"Testy, testy. Did someone not get his nap today?"

No, but he wouldn't give the bear the satisfaction of admitting it. "Shouldn't you be doing something more constructive than taking jabs at my sleeping habits?"

"Probably, but bugging you is more fun."

"I wonder what Miranda would think if she knew you were kicking a poor lion while he's down." Nolan smiled evilly, knowing how Mason feared his pregnant sister-in-law.

"Now that's just mean. Do you know I have to carry around a baggie of carrot muffins in case I run into her? She's freaking nuts these days. Jessie keeps assuring me it's the pregnancy hormones. I hope so, otherwise, once she pops that kid out and goes back to being able to shift into her killer bunny, I might have to move. I'm thinking Alaska."

Nolan chuckled. "As if Jessie will let you guys relocate."

"My swan princess loves me," Mason asserted. Once the most carefree of bachelors, the bear took to married life with gusto, even if he and his father-in-law, the swan king, didn't entirely get along.

"And how is her father?"

"No comment," Mason mumbled.

The FUC agents the bear had brought with him scurried around the place, tagging and bagging items. Nolan couldn't figure out why they bothered. The stuff was junk.

"What's next?" Tired, Nolan's shoulders slumped. What an annoying end to such a promising evening.

"For tonight? Nothing. We'll have the lab run some tests to be certain of the psycho's identity and send some sniffers out on his trail. You're free to leave and find a place to nap because there's no way you can stay here tonight. Probably not for a few nights. You should go stay with your mom."

"I knew you had it out for me, Mason, but that's cruel, even for you."

The bear snickered. "Man, is your mother going to cough up a hairball when she hears about this."

"I'd prefer if we kept this under wraps for as long as possible. The last thing I need is for her to sedate me and to wake up in a padded room for my own protection." Again. Rousing a lioness's protective side never boded well.

"She wouldn't?"

"You don't know her very well then. Trust me, when it comes to her one and only baby boy, nothing is too much."

"I'll do my best to keep this quiet, but she's gonna find out. If I were you, I'd go into hiding now. Bring the bird with you for company and protection."

"Actually, I think you should go to your mother's," Clarice said out of the blue from right behind him.

"Are you insane?" Hmm, probably not his best choice of words given he still planned to try and salvage part of this evening.

"I'm perfectly sane, thank you. And obviously thinking far more clearly than you, sleep deprived one. Given what's happened, and how the psycho got in, your mother is probably your best protection."

"No better than you." *Or me.* He could take care of himself.

"Except I won't be with you. I'm going after this mutant."

"Not alone you're not," he growled.

"Oh yes, I am," she snapped. "Or have you forgotten this is what I do?"

"It's late and you need to rest."

"I'm not tired. And I want to tackle this while the trail is fresh."

"I forbid it."

He didn't need to hear Mason's "Ooh" to know he said the wrong thing.

"Forbid?" Her brow arched. "You don't own me and you're not my superior. I'll do whatever I damned well please to hunt this killer down."

"Clarice." He went to touch her, but she spun out of reach, her long stride taking her into his bedroom. Nolan followed on her heels, trying to stop her. "It's dark. You won't see anything."

"We're in the city. If he's on foot, he might not have gotten far. I might be able to spot him from the air."

The air? She intended to fly? Didn't she grasp the danger? What if someone shot at her? Or she smacked into a window, like thousands of birds did every year?

But Clarice wasn't listening to reason. Ignoring the mess in his room, she ran to his sliding glass doors, shedding clothing as she jogged. He caught a glimpse of toned, pale flesh before she molted, feathers sprouting from her skin. With a leap, she cleared the railing and was airborne. Arms extended, she hung suspended for a moment, and his heart stopped. Then her wings burst into existence, and with a flap that sent a breeze to ruffle his hair, she halted her descent.

She made a magnificent falcon. Sleek in build, and much larger than her non-sentient counterparts, her feathers covered her in a striated blend of gray and brown. She bore the same rapier gaze, which she swept over him for a moment before she swooped off into the dark sky, leaving him clutching the railing, his frustrated roar echoing into the night.

Chapter Thirteen

The lingering vibration of Nolan's roar tingled her skin. In that sound, she heard his frustration, his anger, his fear—*for me.* But she didn't turn back.

She realized the chances of her finding Lester were slim to none. Short of spotting him on a rooftop, there were too many streets with nooks, crannies, and other obstacles for her to perform a proper aerial search, especially at night. Although, maybe she'd get lucky and catch the psycho on a rooftop.

I really need to stop lying to myself.

The real reason she dove off the balcony had little to do with hunting down the mutant and more to do with her, or more specifically, one golden-haired doctor. If it hadn't been for the break-in at his condo, Clarice would have slept with Nolan. Less sleep than doing the wicked, wild, naked, and sweaty, six ways from Sunday. Something about the man got her motor running. Made her forget her task to guard him—or herself. All it took? One touch or look from him and she was ready to tear off his clothes.

It frightened her how little control she seemed to have around him. How easily he'd tunneled through the wall she armored her emotions with. How he consumed her thoughts. Even now, when she should have paid attention to her surroundings and kept her keen eyes on the lookout for Lester, she instead floated aimlessly on the updrafts, her mind whirling with thoughts of *him*.

He wasn't far off the mark when he lamented the ruin of their evening. She regretted the missed opportunity, too. Sure, she understood they didn't have a future together. Their relationship—if you could call their frantic need for each other a relationship—would only last as long as this case did, but she couldn't deny that a teensy tiny part of her wondered what it would be like to belong to man like Nolan. To wake up every day to his smile and tousled, golden hair. What would it be like to belong to his boisterous family whose cracks about ways to baste her made her feel more at home than if they'd treated her with polite respect?

She knew what her sergeant would have said. "You're a weak, bird-brained fool, Clarice. He's a bloody lion. Lions eat falcons like you for breakfast." Mmm, did they ever eat.

Distracted by Nolan's version of eating, she faltered in her flight, her altitude dipping and bringing her precariously close to a mirrored window sky rise. Oops. She flapped her wings and skimmed by, the rush of air momentarily clearing her thoughts.

What should she do? She didn't exactly have any close friends to talk to. Ever since she'd graduated and joined the ASS agency, she'd never stayed in one place long enough to develop friendships. Never had an interest, letting her job consume her time and her life. Oddly enough, she thought of Miranda, the crazy pregnant rabbit, and knew what she'd say. "Go for it! Boink the lion until he roars."

Oh, great bird in the sky, as if she should listen to the advice of a woodland creature, especially of the variety she'd eaten in the past. Still, though, if she were totally honest with herself, she wanted to have sex with Nolan. Wanted to claw at his back, peck at his skin, and just get naked and wild. The only thing holding her back? *Me.*

I'm the one in the way, not the difference in our species, or his mother, or anything else. And for what? She wasn't a virgin. She had no expectation of things going any further. She'd soon leave and wouldn't have to face him every day or deal with his rejection, or worse, indifference. Why not give into the passion? So long as she kept her heart out of it, who would get hurt? No one. And maybe once she let him have his wicked way, the ridiculous ideas floating through her head would stop. And he'd stop putting them there with his ridiculous flirting.

Playing hard-to-get only made him chase her more ardently. Give him what he wanted, which in turn gave her what she wanted, and they could part ways. Easy.

Or course, she'd no sooner decided that and turned around to head back when she saw the scurrying shape on a flat roof. Probably nothing—a human out for a smoke, an animal looking for shelter. Or a pair of escapees dragging an inert body between them.

With a flutter of wings, she alighted on the edge of a building just across from where she saw movement. Still as a stone gargoyle, she assessed the situation.

Furry and bushy-tailed, if much larger and more muscled than normal, it seemed she'd found the squirrely patients. The question was did the body they lugged between them live or not? If not, then the smart thing to do, given she had no weapons other than her claws and beak, was to call for help. The form stirred.

Alive. *Oh, great big steaming pile of pigeon poop.* She mentally cursed as she reassessed her options. If she went for aid, the human would probably end up dead before the cavalry arrived. Alone, though, against two mutant squirrels?

Did she really have a choice?

Besides, she knew a doctor to patch her up.

With a hunting scream that sent mice fleeing, but only caused the giant squirrels to cock their heads, she dove off her perch toward her targets. Lucky her, only one stood its ground while the other scurried to hide. Bad for her, his size wasn't the only thing bigger than normal about him.

Now those are what I call nutcrackers.

At the last moment in her dive, she reared back and let her clawed feet strike first, her talons ripping into fur and knocking her opponent back. He chittered in rage as he flailed, his claws scoring scratches along her legs. With a powerful leap, she bounded up, and then slammed back down, her beak tearing into him as she ducked and weaved, avoiding his overly large teeth. Thankfully, squirrels weren't natural born predators so his fighting ability consisted mostly of snapping teeth and grasping paws. But, it didn't mean he didn't land some blows, some hard enough to bruise later.

Things got a little concerning when his partner, the until now forgotten female, decided to join the fray. She leapt on to Clarice's back with a screech. Unable to shake her off, Clarice did the only thing she could think of. She fell off the edge of the roof. Despite her animal shape, the squirrel let out an all-too-human scream as they plunged, not far, because her mate grabbed her by the tail. As the female squirrel dangled, Clarice broke free and with a few strokes of her wings, which thankfully remained intact if minus a few feathers, took to the air to reassess her foes.

The male squirrel did his best to heave the female back to safety. But the human they'd abducted took that moment to regain consciousness and, his eyes wide with fear, shoved at the male's back. Down went the furry duo. Clarice winced at the splat they made on the pavement below.

Two more psychos down.

Before the human—who almost ended up as dinner—could spot her, Clarice dropped behind him and rapped him on the head. It wouldn't do for him to call the authorities before FUC had a chance to clean up. She almost felt bad for the time he'd probably spend in the psych ward when he regained consciousness and regaled rescuers with a tale about giant mutant squirrels. But, concealment was more important than protecting a human from a few days in a padded room.

The situation more or less contained, she winged away from the scene, taking note of the location first. While her injuries didn't appear life threatening, she did need some help. However, not knowing the city proved a disadvantage. Homing in on the only place she really knew, she flew back to her kitty's condo.

Finding his balcony proved easier than expected, especially given Nolan napped on it wrapped in a sleeping bag. *Is he waiting for me?*

Warmth spread through her. She'd never come home to someone before. Never had anyone who cared enough to wait for her.

Alighting on the concrete floor, she shifted before he deigned to open an eye. She waited for him to say something. Anything.

He didn't say a word as he yawned and stretched. For some reason, his actions annoyed her.

"What are you doing?" she snapped.

"Waiting for you."

His answer mollified her a bit. But he had yet to get up or hug her or…treat her like he cared. She struggled not to let her disappointment show. "I told you to go to your mother's."

He shrugged. "I guess we're both not very good at following orders." Taking a deep inhalation, he frowned at her. "You're injured."

"Just a few scratches."

"A few?" He stood, shrugged off the cocooning shell, and paced around her, his body bristling with tension. "What did you do? Wrestle with a cat?" He growled the last part.

"Actually, it was a pair of squirrels."

He stopped and stood behind her. "Dare I ask why you were playing with squirrels? You know we have some perfectly good restaurants if you're hungry. Or I could have ordered in."

"Eew. I didn't go after them for eating. I caught up with our escaped mutant squirrels. Which reminds me, do you have a phone I can use? We need to call in a cleanup crew."

"Your cell is on the kitchen counter."

Shivering from the evening air and lack of clothing, which he didn't seem inclined to provide, she went through the sliding glass doors and only paused a second as she took in the empty room. "Where's all your stuff?"

"Gone. I had a cleaning crew in while you were out hunting woodland creatures."

"Great big mutant ones, thank you very much."

A rumble at her back told her the distinction didn't sit well. "They cleared everything out, and steam cleaned the carpets."

That explained why her feet were getting wet. The fibers weren't completely dry.

"Quick work."

"The pride might be catty, but they know how to pull together in a crisis."

"What did mommy dearest say?"

"I wouldn't know. I haven't answered her calls."

"And she didn't show up?"

"Oh, she did. However, I was out."

"Out? Out where, you idiot?"

"Looking for you."

He was? Don't melt. Don't melt. Don't… "Do you have any idea how dangerous that was?" she yelled. "What if you ran into Lester or another of the psychos?"

"You mean like you did? Alone?" His quietly spoken words hammered at her harder than a shout would have.

"It wasn't safe and you know it."

"Then I guess you should have stayed to guard me."

The pointed reminder made her wince, and that quickly, her anger dissipated and she changed the subject. "I'm surprised your pride didn't manage to have the place fully furnished too."

"It will be by the end of the day. Furniture stores don't like to deliver after midnight."

Entering the living room, she noted that wasn't entirely accurate as he already had a pair of leather club chairs and an air mattress. Spotting her cell phone on the counter along with a neatly folded pile of clothes, she dialed the FUC switchboard to report on her encounter with the squirrels and their location.

Nolan leaned against the granite top, arms folded over his chest, his expression unreadable. Although, if she were to guess, he simmered. She just couldn't be certain of why he was angry. Yes, she'd left him unguarded, but with a roomful of agents. Agents he'd left to go looking for her? If anyone had a right to anger, it was Clarice.

As soon as she hung up, she made a grab for the clothes, but he caught her hand and shook his head. "Not yet you don't."

"In case you hadn't noticed, I'm naked, and while your condo is warm, I'd prefer to wear some clothes."

"I have noticed. Trust me, I'm doing my best not to do something about it. But you need to shower and let me look at your injuries."

"They're surface wounds. I'll be healed by morning." Or afternoon. She'd lost track of time during her flight.

"Given they were inflicted by my infected patients, we shouldn't assume anything. So hit the shower to clean off and then humor me while I give you a checkup."

Nothing in his tone or expression said he planned anything more than a checkup, yet, a spurt of heat lit low in her belly. She thought back on her conversation with herself and her decision to have fun with the lion. With his grim face and standoffish attitude, had she lost her window of opportunity?

Only one way to find out. With a swing of her hips, she sashayed away toward his bathroom. A barely audible rumble of sound followed. *Perhaps not so disinterested after all.*

But first, a shower, which after catching a whiff of herself, she couldn't deny she needed.

Chapter Fourteen

As soon as she left the room, Nolan whirled around and punched a wall, hard enough to crack the plaster. The pain blossoming across his knuckles did nothing to ease the rage aching for release inside.

She's injured. That didn't sit well with him. Sure, he understood on some visceral level that none of the wounds were grievous, and as she surmised, most would disappear in a few hours. Reasoning didn't calm his agitated lion. An urge to hunt down the scent of the creatures coating her made him punch the wall again. Dead or not, he wanted to kill the squirrels again.

And then, he wanted to mount her. Primitive, yes, but he couldn't help how he felt.

Without the least attempt at modesty, she paraded her nude body before him. Did she not know the torture she inflicted? The self-restraint he had to show not to push her up against a wall and just take her? Nudity might be a fact of life for shifters, and politeness decreed that those who shifted not get ogled. Still, though…a man could only take so much. *And this man can't take anymore.*

To distract himself from the thought of her in the shower, the hot water streaming down her slim, athletic body, her small breasts topped with dark berries, wet and begging for a tongue, he busied himself laying out some basic medical supplies from his medical bag. He'd brought it up from his car when he returned from his futile search for Clarice. His falcon wasn't the only one pissed at him for leaving the safety of his condo and the team in place. He'd returned to find his mother losing her mind. Actually, she probably still ranted, partially out of feat for his safety, but more he suspected because he wouldn't bow to her wishes.

Despite the arguments by his mother, Nolan wouldn't budge from his condo. Clarice had left her stuff behind, which meant she intended to return at some point. If he left, how would she find him? What if she needed him?

Kloe unexpectedly backed him, claiming it was unlikely Lester would return, but just in case, once they'd finished cleaning his place, agents were assigned to watch key entry points. Someone scrounged up an air mattress, along with some clean sheets and a sleeping bag. However, Nolan eschewed the warm comfort inside his home to stand vigil on the balcony—ahem, catnap. He needed the rest, but at the same time as he dozed, his lion side watched, listened, and waited. The moment he heard the flutter of wings, he'd sprang to total awareness, but feigned sleep a moment longer in order to control himself when he caught the myriad scents coming off Clarice, primarily that of her blood.

How he wanted to shake her until he teeth rattled for taking on two of the mutated patients. Who cared if she saved a human? She could have lost her life acting the part of heroine. From the sounds of it, the battle was a close one. *I should have been there to help her.*

And this was the biggest problem he had. Funny enough, it was the same issue he had with his mother. Clarice wanted to do things herself, on her terms. She didn't want anyone to molly coddle her. *Just like me.* For the first time in his life, Nolan understood how hard his mother must have found it to let Nolan forge his own way, face danger by himself, leaving her to worry, worry that maybe everything wouldn't turn out all right.

However, just like he kept forcing his mother to realize he could stand on his own two feet, he also had to realize Clarice was an independent woman. Not just a woman, but an agent, one trained to do a job that would put her in danger on a regular basis. He couldn't set restrictions on her actions. It wasn't up to him to decide what she could or could not do. Whether he liked it or not, he needed to let her make her own choices. Trying to forbid or cage her would cause her to fly. The scary reality was the woman he'd fallen for would never be content to just sit back and let others take the risk. *I guess I'll have to accept this is who she is and make sure I have plenty of antiseptic and bandages on hand for when she comes home.*

Of course, this was all supposing he could convince her to give him a shot and that they could have a future together.

Still unsure of how he would accomplish that, his time for thought ran out as she emerged from the bathroom in a billow of steam, her bare shoulders glistening above the towel she'd wrapped securely around her torso. She arched a brow at his medical array.

"Good grief, Sylvester. I got a few bruises and scratches. I didn't lose a limb."

"Don't be such a noisy chickadee. Zip your protesting beak and get over here." He tempered his taunt with a grin. "Unless the big, bad falcon is scared of a tetanus shot?"

"You just want an excuse to poke me in the butt."

Damn straight he did. "Drop the towel too, would you? I don't want the fibers sticking to any open cuts."

He expected more of an argument. To his shock, the wet terrycloth hit the floor and she undulated her hips as she approached him, the bareness of her mound teasing him, the tautness of her nipples tempting, the half-smile on her lips… Was that an invitation he saw in her eyes?

Mouth suddenly dry, his mind went blank as all the blood in his brain rushed to a certain body part. He stood frozen.

"What are you waiting for?" she asked huskily. "I thought you were going to check me out."

Couldn't she tell he was? And from what he could see, she was perfect. He shook his head and tried to regain some semblance of control before he threw himself on her like a ravening beast. Time to act like a professional. He took note of the bruises on her ribs. The one on her cheekbone. He palpated the skin around them, making sure the bones weren't broken and that she didn't have any internal bleeding. Her sudden indrawn breath made him pause.

"Am I hurting you?"

"Not exactly."

A perfume rose in a seductive cloud to surround him, her desire making itself known. Not pain then. He needed to finish his checkup quickly, make sure she truly was only injured in the most superficial manner. He wouldn't be able to leash himself for long. He placed his hands on her and motioned for her to spin. She presented her back where he found more mottled bruises and minor scratches. He again pressed on the blemished areas, her gasps and hitches of breath coinciding each time with an increase in the heady musk coming from between her thighs.

As she'd said, her wounds were on the surface and would heal in a few hours. The last test he did for pure pleasure.

"Touch your toes."

Over she bent, again without argument, her buttocks pointing, the moist lips of her sex exposed. He ran a finger down her spine from her neck down to the crevice of her cheeks, then between them. A mewl left her as a shudder swept her body.

"Does that hurt?" he whispered.

"Yes."

"Do you want me to fix it?"

"Oh God, yes please."

That was all he needed to hear. Dropping to his knees, he pressed his mouth against her core, his tongue emerging to swipe at her cream. She cried out and shivered. He grasped her cheeks and held her steady as he tongued her, spreading her labia to penetrate her channel and expose her clit. How she responded to his touch. As before, she shook, quivered, and gave in to the passion flaming between them. The more she urged him on, the more frantic his own need became.

Need to have her. Need to claim her. Need to mark her. Need to make her mine.

As she trembled on the brink of orgasm, he couldn't wait any longer. He stood, ripping at his pants when they wouldn't cooperate and slide over his engorged cock, the fabric snagging. Freed, he took himself in hand and rubbed the swollen tip against her moist lips.

"More," she whispered.

Wetting the head, he rubbed himself back and forth against her pussy, applying pressure on her nub.

"Stop teasing me and give me your cock," she growled.

Ever the gentleman, Nolan gave her what she demanded, perhaps a little more forcefully than he meant to. He slammed his dick into her and she yelled. Not in pain. Not in shock. No, his Clarice yelled for more.

"Harder, Nolan. Give it to me. Oh, God. Give it to me hard."

So he did, pounding into her willing flesh, each slap of his body against hers a rhythmic music that brought his own pleasure spiraling higher and higher. His balls tightened and his cock swelled so large it threatened to burst, but he held on, held on until her sex convulsed and spasmed into an orgasm that had her screaming. Screaming his name and her delight. He joined her, roaring her name as his dick spurted.

But his climax was short-lived. The door to his apartment banged open as the men stationed as guards just outside poured in. Whipping around, Nolan, not one hundred percent man in that moment, roared again. "Get out!"

Lucky for them, they did. He snarled in annoyance at his climax cut short.

A giggle had him whipping back around. Clarice stood there, biting her lip, but she couldn't stop a snicker.

"This isn't funny."

"Oh yes it is. You should see the look on your face."

"And what look would that be?"
"The cat who lost his canary."
Then she burst into outright laughter.

Chapter Fifteen

Okay, so maybe Clarice should have tried harder to control her mirth, but who could blame her? The look on his face when those guys barged in? A girl could only hold in so much. She howled with laughter. His perfectly shaped brows drew together in annoyance.

"Evil bird."

"Poor, frustrated kitty," she choked.

"I'll show you who's frustrated."

Nolan stalked toward her with all the feline grace of a predator and she backed up, not out of fear, but because she wanted to prolong the moment. He probably had no idea just how sexy he appeared. His hair crowned him in a wild golden mane, his eyes glowed with irritation—and lust—while his luscious body—with all those glorious muscles—bristled. As for his cock, lo and behold, it stirred, apparently ready for round two. Lucky her.

Enjoying the visual tease, she didn't pay attention to where her retreat led and her heel hit the edge of the air mattress. Teetering, she might have kept her balance, but he took that moment to pounce, his body tackling hers to the bouncy surface, and Clarice braced herself for a balloon pop. To her surprise, the mattress survived, and a good thing, too, given Nolan's body pinned her to it, his hard dick trapped against her lower body, a clear indication of what would come next.

"Is this your way of saying we're not done?" she asked in between his ravenous kisses.

"Not by a long shot," he growled, tugging at her lower lip.

"Good. Get on your back."

"Excuse me?"

"I said get on your back. You've had your turn to explore my body, twice now, I might add. It's my turn to do the same to yours."

She didn't need to ask again. With an ominous creak of plastic, he flipped them on the inflatable bed until she perched atop him. Up she sat, her fingers digging in to the hair covering his chest. Not a hairy beast, he nevertheless possessed a light golden down for her to run her fingers through. He closed his eyes and a rumble shook him as she stroked him.

No way. She paused. "Are you purring?"

He opened one eye to peer at her lazily. "Yes. Is that a problem?"

"No. It's just different."

"Get used to it. A happy kitty purrs."

Her lips curled at his announcement, but he thankfully didn't see as he'd already shuttered his eye. He continued to make his contentment audible and though she would never admit it, it pleased her. But she wanted Nolan more than happy. She wanted to drive him wild. Make him buck and moan her name. Yell at the top of his lungs as he came inside her. Speaking of which…

"You forgot to cover your soldier."

He went still under her. "I did, didn't I?"

Odd how he didn't sound too perturbed. But then again, he'd read her file, which contained her medical records and prescriptions. "I assume you're clean."

"As a whistle."

"Guess it's a good thing I get the shot." As in birth control shot. Clarice didn't indulge in the horizontal mambo often, but when she did, she preferred not to worry.

"Guess so."

"So we're good to go without a hat?"

He sighed noisily and his purring stopped. "Are you just going to talk until you put me to sleep or are you going to do what you promised?"

She tweaked his nipple.

He yelped. "Ouch!"

"Saucy, kitty."

"So punish me."

"I intend to."

The purr came back louder than ever. The vibration shook his entire body, which meant her sex, pressed against his hard lower belly, also felt the effect—and quite enjoyed it. She caught his lower lip between her teeth and nibbled as his hands spanned her waist. Slender-fingered and smooth at the tips, his digits tickled her skin instead of abrading it. No wonder they felt so good when they touched her lower parts. The lack of callouses an advantage to his being a doctor instead of a tradesman.

As she kissed him, savoring the roughness of his tongue and the lingering taste of her own body, she let her hands stroke up and down his muscled arms. She skimmed every part of him, learning his shape, the nuances of his skin, where he caught his breath, what made him twitch. She explored all of his upper body, pinching his nipples lightly and laughing softly into his mouth when his hips jerked.

She felt the hot prod of his dick against the crease of her buttocks. Insistent and ready, he tried to subtly guide her over it, but she held him back. She'd not finished her exploration quite yet. With one last suck of his lower lip, she broke the kiss so she could crawl backward down his body until she straddled his thighs.

Erect, thick, and long, his cock lay against his lower body amidst a nest of golden curls. She grasped it and stroked its silky length, brushing her thumb over the tip and rubbing the glistening pearl into the head. He rumbled. "Now who's driving who crazy?"

"You ain't seen nothing yet," she drawled before dipping down to take him in her mouth. Clarice didn't give head often, but she might just make an exception for the man beneath her. Oh, how he made it into a treat. Every suction of her mouth, every lick of her tongue, every slide of her lips up and down his length evoked a reaction. He moaned, groaned, thrashed, and bucked. He showed such enjoyment in her touch, such pleasure she couldn't help but enjoy herself too. Her pussy moistened, then ached, her own arousal pulsing in time to his cries. Responding to his evident excitement.

For a moment, she thought about taking him all the way, of letting him come into her mouth, but selfish need stayed her ravenous lips. She released him, slick and erect, to poise herself over him. His eyes opened, his lids at half-mast. Oh, how sexy he looked. And at the same time, so hungry.

She meant to ease herself onto him slowly, to impale herself on his length, inch by inch. But he grabbed her about the hips and yanked her down, sheathing himself in a fluid motion that had her head flinging back and her fingers digging into his chest.

"Oh hell yeah!" she cried. He filled her to perfection. Stretched her and pulsed within her channel. Every slight movement, every grind of her hip, rotation of her pelvis, every twitch of his cock, went through her like a jolt. And the entire time she ground herself against him, rocking in a slow rhythm that had her pleasure mounting, he hissed, "Yes! Yes! Yes! Give it to me. Come for me. Squeeze me."

She gave it to him all right. With a shattering cry, she came on his cock, the waves of her climax gripping and milking his shaft until spent. She would have collapsed on him, a heaving and boneless mess, but he wasn't done.

Hands still spanning her waist, he took his turn, lifting and dropping her on his hard dick. Each slam made her cry out. Spasm. Shudder. Up. Down. Up. Down. Over and over he pushed into her, hitting a sweet spot inside, her oh-so-sensitive g-spot, which in turn, made her sex tighten once more, to want…to prepare for…

"Oh. Dear. God." She screamed as she came for the third time, or meant to. Her orgasm came upon her so powerfully she opened her mouth wide, but couldn't find the breath to actually release it, the moment proved so intense. Nolan, on the other hand, had plenty of lung capacity left and he roared. God, did he roar, the vibration of it prolonging her orgasm.

This time, no one interrupted them and he got to fully enjoy himself, so much so that his claws popped out and pricked her skin. Not for long. He must have realized what he did because he released her waist and dug at the sheets beneath them.

POP!

The hiss of escaping air as their temporary bed deflated brought on the giggles again. Twice in one evening. It had to be a new record for her.

"Don't laugh." He sounded so disgusted.

She snickered.

"This isn't funny."

She chuckled.

Nolan sighed. "You know, I'm really usually much more suave than this."

"What, you mean you don't usually have people barge in during the middle of sex and have mattresses go flat? I guess that makes me special."

The arms he wrapped around her squeezed tight. "Very special."

His words took her by surprise, especially since she heard the sincerity in them. But then again, they'd just had great sex. Still, though, she wanted to ask what made her special? Was it something he said to all his conquests? *Or am I different?*

"I can feel your mind whirling," he said.

"You cannot."

"Can too. For once, just relax and enjoy yourself."

"But—"

"Go to sleep, Clarice."

"I don't know if I can." She'd never felt more alive. Happier. She didn't want the feeling to end. Didn't want the moment to end. She wouldn't examine the reason why. She didn't want to ruin it. Not when she feared what it meant.

This means nothing. It was just good sex. Just ask her body, which still thrummed from the pleasure. Pressed against his chest, she didn't move to get off, even if she wasn't usually much of a cuddler. He nuzzled at her hair, and lo and behold, if he didn't start to purr again. She thought about making a comment, but the sound soothed her, lulled her, and slumber swept her into its grip.

Chapter Sixteen

Waking up with her cheek pressed to Nolan's chest, the steady thud of his heartbeat a smooth, soothing cadence proved a new experience. Clarice didn't sleep with her bed partners. She didn't cuddle. And she most especially didn't lie splayed across them like a downy eiderdown, so relaxed and content she didn't want to move.

What is happening to me?

They'd had sex. Great sex. So why did a part of her long to kiss the stubble on his chin? Why did she want to wiggle her hips and see if something would wake up and give her a *good morning*? Why did she want to stay pressed against him, cozy and warm when there was a job to do?

The conclusion stole her breath.

Oh no, I'm starting to care for him. Just the mere thought, the frightening idea, caused her heart to flutter in panic. No. She couldn't fall for the lion. They were too different. He was too high maintenance. His mother was a nut job—a fun nut job, but still, crazier than a loon. Clarice didn't belong with him, in his world. She had a job, an apartment, a life—of sorts—back in her own city.

But nothing to really prevent me from staying. No one to care if I never went back. She could remain here, start a new life, if she wanted. *If he wanted me to.*

What total, utter insanity. Nolan wasn't about to ask her to stay and become his what? Girlfriend? Bedmate? Occasional hop-in-the-sack-buddy? The guy was a slut and like an idiot, she'd allowed great sex to make her think she felt something more.

She wanted to slap herself and then shake herself silly for falling for his act. Rolling off him, she heard him mumble, his arm reaching for her to draw her back in. She evaded it and whispered, "I have to go to the bathroom." And she did. For a cold shower and a dose of reality.

No matter how pleasurable the sex, Clarice needed to remember she was only here temporarily. Once she'd completed her mission, her time with the lion would end.

Now if only the reality check didn't hurt so much. Unable to face him, not yet with her realization so fresh, she slipped from his condo, leaving him to slumber under the protection of the FUC agents placed outside in the hall.

The sooner she got the job done, the sooner she could escape the clutches of the feline who made her wish for things she could never have. *A home and his heart.*

*

Nolan woke alone with only a vague recollection of Clarice leaving their deflated bed. What she claimed was a need to use the washroom was apparently an excuse to go out investigating, without him, again.

Despite his realization the night before that he couldn't forbid her from facing danger, it still rankled. Worrying about the safety of someone he cared about truly sucked, however, if he was going to convince her to let him into her life, he needed to accept it. *I just don't have to like it.*

Breakfast, a shower, and a drive to work later, he still felt an urge to grumble. More than once, he'd grabbed his phone, tempted to call her just to hear her voice. Each time he set it down and chastised himself for acting so needy.

I am a lion. Haughtiness was his middle name. Still, would it have killed her to leave him a note? Send him a text? Something?

It irritated him to realize he had no idea when he'd get to see her again. He just knew he would. *She won't escape me that easily.*

It mollified him somewhat to discover Clarice met up with some other agents to go over the items found in the squirrel's lair—mostly bags and bags of nuts. Surely she'd remain safe enough doing something so mundane. He would have liked to join her; however, fate, also known as his boss, possessed other plans. Apparently, FUC had other tasks to keep him busy.

It wasn't only he and his falcon who enjoyed a busy night. His escaped patients kept the FUC staff on duty hopping. The escaped ostrich and gecko, who paired up in the outside world, turned themselves in to some agents. Life on the street, and their new condition, didn't agree with them. Unlike the other mutants they'd run into, the escaped duo retained enough of their sanity to realize they needed help.

It made Nolan wonder if perhaps some of the others could be salvaged as well. Or so he argued. But, those passing down the edicts wouldn't budge. No chances were to be taken with those still on the loose. However, Nolan did win one concession. Kloe ordered Nolan to evaluate the physical and mental state of the pair who'd returned and were currently jailed in a holding cell at the FUC office.

While he conducted interviews and ran some tests, he heard through the grapevine that they'd recovered the body of another patient, but not before some human with a camera got a video clip and posted it on YouTube. Luckily, people treated it much as they would a Nessie and Big Foot sighting. In other words, a bunch chattered excitedly about it being proof of alien life while others scoffed and called it the worst Photoshop job they'd ever seen. Meanwhile, the body itself got accidentally "lost" on its way to the human morgue. Another FUC cover-up to keep the humans in the dark.

All in all, he spent an eventful day with only one nap to tide him over. Of Clarice, he didn't see beak or feather until he returned home, accompanied by Viktor who drove while Nolan slept. The croc nudged him awake when they got to the underground garage. Nolan's gaze immediately honed in on the empty parking spot alongside his. No parked Goldwing, which meant no Clarice.

"Why the dour face, doc?" the croc asked as he escorted Nolan to his floor where FUC agents still stood guard.

I wonder what the neighbors think. He wondered even more where Clarice was and if she was all right. He roused himself from his musings to answer Viktor, speaking his thoughts aloud. "Why must women be so pigheaded?"

"Because they know it drives us nuts."

"So you mean Renee does that to you too? Goes diving into danger and doesn't call to let you know she's okay?"

"Uh no, but apparently I do that on a regular basis. It scares her, which in turn, pisses her off, not that she says so."

"How does she handle it?"

"Why the questions?"

"Because I need some advice, and I'd rather not listen to that of the female members of my pride."

Grunting, Viktor swung open the apartment door. "Can't blame you there. How does my wife handle my job? Let's just say I do on purpose sometimes make my day seem more eventful than it is and leave it at that."

It took Nolan only a moment to decipher his meaning. "You mean you putting yourself in danger brings you *closer*?"

"If you mean as in clothing optional closer, then yes. But if you tell anyone, I'll kill you." The killer glint in the croc's eye didn't hold any mirth.

"I won't say a word." Nolan valued his life too much. "If you don't mind me asking another question, how did you know you loved her?"

"What is this, the Dr. Phil hour? Is this about that falcon the office has you shacking up with?"

"Maybe."

A knowing smirk crossed Viktor's face. "It is. Ha. And people think my fox and I make an odd couple."

"Clarice and I aren't so odd. We're both predators."

Viktor snorted. "That's a thin comparison, doctor, and you know it. But as to your question—if you're asking what it will take to get her to love you, then I don't know. She's a tough bird, that one. And I'll bet she doesn't trust easy. I know I don't, nor am I into that sappy, lovey-dovey crap."

"Yet you love Renee."

"Listen, doc. I fought real hard against having feelings of any kind for my fox. Real hard. But she just wouldn't take no for an answer. I almost lost her I was so damned stubborn. Lucky for me, she never gave up."

"In other words, I should keep trying."

"I'm not saying nothing. Who knows what's going on in that bird's brain? But if you care for her…" Viktor shrugged. "Hell, don't ask me. I don't know how to romance a woman or make flowery speeches. You should ask Mason or someone who's good with words."

Big mouth Mason? Not happening, not unless he wanted it posted on every FUC message board. "I think I'll pass. Actually, you've been most helpful."

"I have? Don't tell anyone." Viktor tossed him a glower. "I don't need every lion, tiger, and cougar coming to me for advice. I'm a soldier, not some bloody dating shrink."

"Your secret is safe with me."

With a grunt, Viktor left his condo, but not before checking every nook and cranny to ensure no psychos lurked. As Viktor tucked his gun in his waistband, Nolan could see the disappointment on the croc's face when nothing popped out to attack. There was a man who loved his job.

Alone, Nolan wandered around his condo, noting the new furniture and clean smell. All traces of the attack were gone, even the holes he had punched in the wall, erased by a coating of plaster and paint. But more interesting than his new décor were the shopping bags filled with women's clothing and toiletries.

Hope lit a fire inside his chest. If someone went shopping for Clarice and left her things here, it meant she planned to return.

Whistling, Nolan planned his assault. When Clarice arrived just as dusk fell, through the front door this time and not the balcony, and wearing an unfortunate amount of clothing, he was prepared.

Candles flickered. The table sat ready with a dinner for two. Flowers adorned several vases. The food chilled in the fridge. Nolan greeted her with a glass of wine and a bright smile. "How was your day?"

For a moment, panic flitted across her face. He froze lest the slightest move send her flying. Clarice eyed him and the room suspiciously. She took one cautious step, then another.

"What is this?" She flapped a hand at the place setting for two.

"Supper. I ordered us some sushi with rice."

"Sushi?" Her eyes lit up and he wanted to fist pump at having gotten something right.

"From the best place in town. Sit down while I grab it from the fridge."

When he returned with the two large platters he ordered earlier, he found her perched on a chair, fingers toying with her wine glass, her expression indecipherable. Not exactly the warm kiss and hug he'd hoped for, but at least she'd not fled. However, given the tenseness of her body, he knew he should tread carefully.

"Here you go." He set the offering down with a flourish and took a seat across from her. "I wasn't sure what kind of fish you liked best, so I ordered a little bit of everything."

"What are you up to, Sylvester?" she asked suspiciously.

"Me? Nothing."

"This isn't nothing. This looks like a guy trying to score."

He laughed. "Okay. You caught me. Can you blame me, though? Last night was incredible, and I'm a selfish lion. I want a repeat." Why bother lying? He knew she valued the truth and the truth was, he found her desirable. What woman didn't want to hear that?

"You could have just asked. You didn't need to put on this show."

"What show? I need to eat. You need to eat. Got to keep our energy up for the evening's entertainment."

"Pretty sure of yourself, aren't you? Who says I want seconds?"

"I do. And thirds. And fourths."

A ghost of a smile finally curled her lips. "You are something else, Sylvester."

"Why thank you, Clarice. I'll take that as a compliment. Now eat or I'm going to skip the main course altogether and go straight for dessert."

Arching a brow, she took a sip of her wine before asking, "And what decadent treat do you have in store for dessert?"

"I'm in the mood for some cream. Hot, delicious, thighs around my neck cream."

Mmm, now there was the reaction he waited for. Her pupils dilated. She licked her lips, and leaned back in her chair, letting her legs fall apart. Even with the several feet between them, the invitation seemed clear. His nose quivered, but it was her huskily murmured, "Why wait?" that sent him diving from his chair.

As for the rug burn on his knees, which he noted hours later when they finally got around to eating a late supper? Totally worth it.

*

Over the next two weeks, he and Clarice fell into a routine. During the day, they tackled their separate tasks, her investigating while he dealt with his mutant patients. Of Lester, the psycho who'd trashed his place, not a sign did they find. Actually, since the day after that fateful evening, all the remaining escaped patients seemed to have disappeared in thin air.

The sightings stopped. The homeless remained on the streets begging. The missing persons bulletin board didn't acquire new names, and no humans ended up at the morgue with bite marks. And stray animals everywhere probably breathed a sigh of relief.

Things went more or less back to normal. One by one, FUC cut back guard details as agents returned to their regular day jobs. It seemed the worst of the crisis had passed. Speculation led to several theories, one being that the remaining patients at large adjusted and blended back in to real life, or their mutations killed them at last. Either way, people relaxed and let down their tense guard.

Despite the lack of action in the field and at work, Nolan had never been happier. While he disliked his separation from Clarice during the day, he couldn't deny he loved the nights. It became the most natural thing in the world for he and Clarice to sit down to a nicely catered dinner and talk, followed by hot lovemaking that didn't always make it to a bed.

Over the course of those uneventful days, he got to know Clarice, and fell more and more in love. Truly in love. It wasn't just about the great sex, he loved the woman, every ornery, bossy inch of her. He just didn't admit it to her. Couldn't, because despite her opening up and telling him about her life in the orphanage and the shenanigans she put up with in the ASS office, and him returning the favor and regaling her with stories of growing up molly coddled by an overprotective lioness, he feared her reaction. While she didn't seem to mind their current living arrangement, nothing she did or said indicated in any way that she wanted it to become permanent.

Oddly enough, his boss forced him to realize he needed to do something about the situation before it was too late.

Kloe called him into her office late Friday afternoon, almost three weeks after Clarice joined the FUC team. She motioned for him to sit. "Thank you, Nolan, for coming."

"Anytime. I take it you want an update on the patients?" And by patients, he referred to the pair who'd turned themselves in for voluntary testing.

"Yes, please."

"I've made no progress in reversing the mutations in Ellie or Joey. The good news, though, is that they've responded well to the hormone therapy, and the adrenaline spikes they were experiencing, which led to their bouts of rage, are now under control."

"So no more murderous rampages?"

"Well, seeing as how they never killed anyone during their short period of freedom, I'd say that was never an issue to begin with." Not unless non-sentient field mice counted. If they did, then a lot of shifters were in trouble.

"But can they be trusted to enter the real world?"

"If you're asking if they need to remain incarcerated, then in my professional opinion? No. I would still like them to come in for weekly checkups to keep an eye on them, but other than that, I don't think they're any more dangerous than Renee or Miranda."

Kloe made a face. "That's not reassuring."

Nolan chuckled. "Sorry."

"I'll give them the good news tonight then and make arrangements for them to receive proper housing and set them up with jobs. I think Joey might make a great agent. I was thinking of pairing him with Viktor and letting him mentor him."

"I think Joey would really like that. But Viktor? Not so much."

"I know." A wicked grin crossed his boss's lips. "Now, as for the rest of the escaped patients...there's still no sign of them. Either they're dead, gone deep into hiding, or behaving. Whatever the case, the higher ups have ordered us to go back to our regular routine. We're pulling the remaining guards off you and your staff, which in turn, means I have no reason to keep Clarice from returning to ASS."

"What?" He bolted up in his seat. "You're sending her back?"

"I have to. Remember, she was only here on a loan basis. Her commanding officer called me, today as a matter of fact, and demanded her return since we've hit a dead end in our investigation and shifter hunt."

"But she can't go. I still need her," he blurted without thinking.

"Do you feel threatened? Are you aware of something I'm not?" Kloe's brows drew together in concern.

"No… That is… You see…" Flustered, Nolan sought the right words. And couldn't find an excuse that wouldn't sound stupid. So he settled for the truth. "I might have kind of fallen in love with her."

"I see. Is this your way of asking if we could use her services at the office?"

"I hadn't thought that far ahead. I guess she might like that."

Leaning forward, Kloe pinned him with her gaze. "You guess? Nolan, is she aware of your feelings?"

"I don't know. Maybe. I haven't exactly told her."

"Why not?"

He squirmed. "Because I'm a cowardly lion."

Kloe barked out a laugh. "You? Cowardly? I doubt it. I've seen you face down the agents in this office without batting an eye, including Viktor. You took on that monster in the sewer with no care for your own safety. And do you know how many people sweated bullets when you decided to interview Ellie and Joey in person instead of behind the bullet proof glass?"

"Yeah, but that's not the same."

"You have plenty of courage, Nolan. What you're experiencing right now is a fear of rejection. Don't tell me you've never had it happen before?"

A sheepish grin pulled his lips. "Um, no actually. I guess you could say Clarice is my first real love."

Kloe's mouth rounded into an O of surprise. "No way."

"Yes way. I mean, don't get me wrong. I've been with lots of women. Dated some even for more than a few months, but Clarice is the first one I've ever felt something for. The only one I've ever dreamed of a future with. I don't know what I'll do if I tell her and find out she doesn't feel the same way." Maybe take up yowling at night in the alley like the other tomcats.

"Well, if I were you, I'd tell her quick, because if you don't, she's going to leave."

"I need more time. Can't you tell her ASS boss that you still need her?"

"I'm sorry, Nolan. I wish I'd known before, then maybe I could have done something, but now, unless she chooses to stay, it's kind of out of my hands."

With those words, Nolan knew he had to act. No more putting it off. Time to tell Clarice how he felt. Today.

But when he got home and saw the note on the table, his sinking heart told him he'd waited too long. He didn't need to see her crisp, "Thanks for everything, Sylvester," to know she flew the coop, taking his heart with her.

His mournful meow didn't make him feel better, and for once, napping didn't solve all his problems. So he resorted to what his cousins did when dealing with heartbreak; he ordered up a huge tub of catnip flavored ice cream and proceeded to get tipsy.

Chapter Seventeen

The soft click of his door closing woke him from where he lay splayed on his couch, face down, wet from the drool on the fancy throw cushion acting as a pillow.

Soft steps approached and his interest perked. With his face buried, he couldn't smell who visited, but he knew who he hoped for. Clarice. Had she returned? He rolled over, eager to see the woman he missed. One glance and dejection set back in. "Oh. It's you."

"Well hello to you too, son," drawled his mother. "Could you act any happier to see me?"

"I was hoping you were someone else." Someone he'd not seen or heard from in three days. Three. Long. Days. Depressed, he'd called in sick to work and moped in his condo, eating and sleeping, trying to fathom how he could have fallen so hard—and how she could have left without even saying goodbye. *Without even giving me a chance to convince her to stay.*

"Why haven't you answered your phone? I've been calling."

"I know." Each time, he'd pounced on his cell phone hoping to hear something from the falcon who'd stolen his heart only to sink further in depression when it wasn't her. It occurred to him to call her first, but what could he say? *Hey Clarice. I miss you. Will you come back?* Do-r-k-y! He didn't think he could stand it if she hung up on him, or worse, laughed.

His mother planted her hands on her hips, her mouth a taut line of annoyance. "If you knew I was calling, why didn't you answer?"

"Because I didn't feel like it."

"What is wrong with you? Is this about that stupid bird?"

"She's not stupid."

"Matter of opinion. Why are you moping?"

"I don't mope. Moping is for pussies."

"Says the man lying around in his boxers with cartons of empty ice cream littered around him."

Not just ice cream, but pizza too. Classic comfort food, or so all the breakup articles he'd read assured. "I was hungry." But no amount of food filled the hole in his heart.

"Don't lie to your mother. You fell for that overgrown chicken, didn't you?"

Fell hard, and now couldn't seem to muster the interest to get back up. *How pathetic am I?* "And if I did?" He pushed himself to a seated position, peeling the candy bar wrapper from his bare chest and ignoring the spoon that dangled by his ear, caught in his unwashed mane.

"Forget the bird. She's not right for you. You're a lion, Nolan. King of the beasts. A noble creature meant for great things."

"I am doing great things already, Mother. I help save lives. I make a difference. And who cares what species I am? It's what's inside here," he thumped his chest, his hand coming away sticky, "that counts, not the purity of my bloodline."

"A bloodline that goes back generations."

"Yeah, so you keep reminding me. I hate to break it to you, Mother, but I don't care. And neither should you. I want love."

"Love is overrated."

"According to you and yet, aren't you the one who never remarried after Dad passed away?" An unfortunate safari gone horribly wrong when Nolan was just a baby.

"I never found the right lion to take his place."

"And I never found the right lioness."

"Maybe if we looked to the western prides—"

"I don't need to look. I already found. And she's not a lion. She's not a cat. Nor does she come with a dowry or political leverage."

"Then what does she give you?"

"Happiness. She makes me happy. Doesn't that count for something?" He asked this with all seriousness. He could respect tradition and a need for continuity where their heritage was concerned, but his cousins had already produced more than enough cubs to ensure their line would continue.

"You'd choose your own wellbeing over that of the pride?" His mother arched a brow.

Would he? He looked at his mother, thought of the lionesses and tigresses she'd paraded in front of him over the course of his life. None ever made him feel as if his world rested in their paws. None made the sun seem brighter. None made him happy like his falcon did. Did his mother deserve the grandchildren she so ardently desired? Yes, and she could have them if she would let go of her prejudice against other species. And with that, his answer shone so clearly. "I love Clarice, Mom, and that's that. I know it's not what you or the pride wanted. Hell, it's not what I expected, but I can't help what I feel. I love her, bird or not, and nothing you say can make me change my mind. So get used to it. You're going to have a falcon as a daughter-in-law." Reality came crashing back. "Or you would have if she hadn't left me."

"Excellent."

"You don't have to be so darned smug about the fact she dumped me." His shoulders slumped as he pouted. Spotting a half-eaten chocolate bar, he snagged it and chewed the sugary treat.

"I'm not pleased about that part. I said excellent because I think Clarice will make a fine daughter-in-law. About time you found a woman to settle down with."

He almost choked on a peanut. "Hold on a second. What did you say?"

"I said I think Clarice is a fine choice."

Nolan blinked. Scratched his itchy scalp. Slapped his ears, both sides. Shook his head and winced when the spoon caught in the tangles swung and bopped him in the nose. He yanked it out with a few golden strands before clearing his throat to say, "Sorry, but can you repeat that. I thought I heard you say that you think Clarice will make a fine choice. We are talking about the same woman, right? ASS agent. Avian background. The one you get into a fight with every time you run into her."

"One and the same."

Hallucination. Had to be, brought on by excessive consumption of sugar and catnip. He threw himself back down on the couch. "I need to go back to sleep," he mumbled, his face buried in his drool dampened pillow.

"You've slept enough. It's time you stopped wallowing in self pity and did something to get her back."

Nolan turned his face and opened an eye to regard his mother. "Let's back up a step. Since when do you like her? Last I heard you scream, you hated Clarice because she is, and I quote, 'A bird-brained, scrawny little pigeon.' "

"Reverse psychology, son." His mother patted his cheek. "If I'd said I liked her and treated her nicely, you would have run the other way."

"Would not have."

"Yes, you would have because you delight in doing the opposite of what I tell you. You have since you were little."

"Because you're bossy."

"Yes, I am. And so is Clarice. You know, in many respects, she reminds me a lot of me."

Nolan gagged. "Oh God, don't say that. You'll ruin everything."

"Don't be such a kitten. I didn't mean physically; after all, the woman is a string bean. I meant mentally. She's strong willed. Courageous and unwilling to put up with crap. An excellent markswoman. Perfect for my spoiled baby cub."

"I am not spoiled."

"Says the man who still thinks his underwear gets magically washed when he leaves it on the floor."

"Oh, I know who is taking care of my laundry. I'm not stupid. Why do it myself when you're all so willing to do it for me?" A ghost of a smile touched his lips.

"Where did I go wrong?" his mother lamented. Up went her hands in a dramatic gesture that had him rolling his eyes. She caught the expression and shook her finger. "Impertinent boy."

"Hey, you raised me."

"I did. Despite what you think, or what I think the pride needs, ultimately, I do want you to be happy."

"You have a funny way of showing it," he grumbled.

"So sue me for being overprotective. One day, when you have your own children, you'll understand."

His depression settled back over him. "Kind of hard to get started on that when the woman I love has flown away."

"And you're just going to let her go?"

"What else do you expect me to do?"

"So that's it? You're just going to give up. I thought you cared for her."

"I do."

"I thought you were willing to fight for her?"

"I am!"

"Then stop acting like such a pussy. You're a bloody lion. Act like one. Stalk her skinny butt down, pin her with a paw, and pluck her feathers until she admits she loves you."

"Um, Mom, I want her to love me, not kill me, or have me arrested for assault."

"Stupid laws. Fine. Do it the modern way. Text her, or call her and tell her you miss her. Ask her to come back. Admit how you feel. But for God's sake, don't give up without a fight."

His mother was right—ack, how he hated to admit it. Why did he give up so easily? He'd known from the start getting Clarice to care for him would be fraught with challenge. It was time for him to act, but to call her up and declare he loved her? No. Too impersonal. *I need to do this in person. Face to face. Or on my knees—maybe while tonguing her.* She could never manage to say no when he did that.

He sprang up from the couch. "You know what? You're right. I should track her down so I can tell her how I feel." Kiss her senseless. Make love to her until she promised him anything, even a lifetime together. "Where are my car keys?"

"Um, Nolan?"

"What?" he asked absently as he stalked through the empty ice cream cartons and pizza boxes, on the hunt for his keys.

"You might want to take a shower first. Run a comb through your hair. Find some shoes. Maybe put some pants on. You know, clean yourself up. You're kind of rank."

Catching a glimpse of himself in the hall mirror, he did a double take. Oh boy, who was the wild-eyed, shaggy-haired beast with bloodshot eyes? Mother was right. Again. Argh!

Shower first. Clothes. Then he'd go after his falcon and he wouldn't stop stalking her until she gave in. So what if she'd left? He'd erred in not declaring his feelings. He knew how stubborn she was, how proud. He also knew from the way she'd opened up to him and let him in on her secrets that she had to care. Clarice wouldn't have let him get so close if she didn't. And if she wasn't ready to admit her undying affection for him, then by damn, he'd keep whittling at her resolve until she finally caved into pressure and grudgingly conceded.

His mother left with a promise to return shortly with a battalion of cleaners. But he planned to be gone already.

Whistling in his shower, a strong soap washing away the traces of depression, he planned what he would say. Nothing seemed just right. I love you seemed too straight forward, but a long speech? He could just imagine her disdainful smirk. He could try kissing Clarice senseless and when she got to the point where she liked to scream, "Yes!" pop the question, and trick her. However, he doubted that would go over well later on when she came down from her climatic high.

Rinsing off, his nose wrinkled as the scent of stale popcorn wafted over him. Odd, because he didn't recall eating any during his self-pity stint. A moment later, his eyes widened in realization, but before his lazy lion could surge to the rescue, something hard conked him over the head, and Nolan slumped to the shower stall floor, a ring of mini Clarices fluttering around his unconscious head.

Chapter Eighteen

When she'd made her impromptu decision to flee the coop, chickening out on saying goodbye to her lion, Clarice thought she'd made the right decision. She truly had. *We don't belong together*, no matter what her heart thought.

And what did her heart think? It loved the stupid lion. Probably had for longer than she cared to admit. But loving him didn't mean she'd resort to begging to stay with him or holding out for crumbs of his affection.

Not Clarice. Pride wouldn't let her. The same way she wouldn't show how much she longed for someone to adopt her when she was young, she didn't dare show Nolan how she wanted something more. How a part of her fantasized about them staying together forever and popping out little hatchlings, or even fuzzy little cubs, of becoming a family.

Despite understanding their time together was temporary, she soaked in the pleasure of having someone to come home to, who cared about her day, who listened to what she had to say, who made her feel important. Loved. Nolan played the part of caring partner so well that she lived the fantasy while she could, and loved the stupid feline while she had a chance.

When the time came to say goodbye? She couldn't do it to his face, fearful she'd break down and beg him for something he'd never offered. A happily forever after.

Melancholy clogging her throat, she gathered her things and left while he was at work. Her note, one line of meaningless nothing instead of the several lengthy ones she'd torn up, a feeble thank you for what they'd shared. But what else could she do? Everything else she wrote sounded so…so clingy. So desperate. So needy.

Tears in her eyes—dust, had to be dust—she boarded a bus for home, leaving behind the Goldwing she adored, the life she'd come to cherish, and the man she loved even more.

Mistakenly, she'd thought once she got home and fell back into her regular routine that things would go back to normal, that she'd go back to normal; cold, acerbic, and uncaring. Instead, she found herself turning when she caught a glimpse of gold from the corner of her eye. Listened for a roar that never came. And more pathetic, even went window-shopping for a kitten.

Thankfully, sanity prevailed before she bought a little furball, but it just made her loneliness more acute, which was why she wasn't paying much attention when her boss—the same prick who'd assigned her to FUC in the first place—reamed her out for something. She couldn't have said what. It might have been for not paying attention on the job, which she was currently guilty of as he droned on and on. She couldn't have cared less as she peered out the window, eyes scanning the parking lot yet again for a dark grey Audi.

Dammit. Why can't I stop thinking of him?

Her cellphone rang and she peered at the screen. The caller ID had her spine stiffening. She cut off her ASS boss midsentence. "I need to answer this."

"Don't you dare. I'm talking to—"

Clarice turned her back on him. "Hey, Garfield. Miss me already? Your catty friends not giving you the exercise you need?" She taunted Brenda, faintly smiling for the first time in days.

"Clarice. Thank God I got you. I need you. More specifically, Nolan needs you."

He did? For a moment, elation made her heart stutter, then she came back to earth. "Needs me? Then he's got a funny way of showing it. I mean, really, getting his mom to call me?"

"Oh stuff it, bird. Despite what you might think, Nolan's been a wreck since you left."

"He has? Why?"

"I don't know how you managed it, but my fool son fell in love with you. Told me his happiness is more important than his duty to the pride and that it hinges on being with you. He insists he wants to spend his life with you."

"He does?" She whispered the two words before clearing her throat and finding a vestige of her pride. "If he cares so much, then why hasn't he called?"

"Because he's a stubborn idiot, just like you."

"I don't believe you. Prove it. Put him on the phone." She so wanted to hear his voice, to believe his mother when she said he missed her.

"I can't."

"Why not?"

"Because he's been kidnapped, you chattering magpie."

"What? Why didn't you tell me?" Clarice yelled.

"I was trying, but you kept nattering."

"When? How long?" Despite her panic at the news, she tried to focus on the important facts.

"An hour or so. He was getting ready to come find you, as a matter of fact, when he was attacked. We found traces of blood in his shower."

Blood? Her lion was injured. Clarice paced. "Who took him? Do we have any clues?"

"None really other than a kernel of corn and some hair we believe came from that psycho called Lester."

Her heart stuttered. That wasn't good. "But there wasn't enough blood at the scene to signal a fatality?"

"According to Mason, he thinks the mutant knocked Nolan out and took him somewhere. We just don't know where. I need you to find him, Clarice. Please find my baby boy."

Even without the please, Clarice would have gone, but the broken note in Brenda's voice brought tears to her eyes. "I'll find him," she promised. "I'm on my way."

She hung up just as her ASS boss grabbed her by the arm. "Oh no you're not. I don't know who you think you are, but as an employee of this office, you can't just walk off whenever you like or ignore me when I'm talking to you."

Clarice glared down at the hand gripping her. "Let go of me."

"Or what?"

"Or I'll break your fingers."

"Do that and I'll have your job, Avian Union or not."

"I don't want your job." She peeled off his hand, smiling coldly at his wince.

"You walk out of here and you're done with ASS."

She cocked her head and smirked. "Good, because you know what I learned during my time away? FUC is better. Definitely more satisfying. Why, I'd even go so far as to say that FUC is way better than ASS. I quit." And with those words, she pivoted on her heel and left.

She had a lion to save. A man to kiss silly. And a confession to make. *Time to stop being a stubborn chicken and tell him how I feel.*

So what if she and Nolan belonged to two different worlds? She loved him and it was time she admitted it. Now, if only he could hold on long enough for her to rescue him and tell him herself.

I'm on my way, Sylvester. And she was ready to kick some serious mutant butt.

Chapter Nineteen

Nolan returned to consciousness only to wish he'd remained napping. Every part of him hurt and it only took a moment for him to remember why. Or parts of it, anyway.

Lester surprised him in his shower. Embarrassing, to say the least. *Some predator I am.* In his defense, he'd not expected the attack. Still, though, his lion should hang its head in shame. A chimp one-upping a jungle cat? Mason would never let him live it down.

Of course, that presupposed he'd survive his current dilemma. Bleak didn't come close to describing it. Currently, he found himself strapped to a table in some kind of poorly lit storage room, a rather freaky one that made him wonder if he hallucinated, as props from various movies towered around him, from an eight-foot tall hobbit to a gun-wielding action hero. It took him several blinking moments to realize he looked upon the remnants of movie marketing. Posters hung on the walls, overlapping each other, the corners curling in many cases. Cardboard cutouts ranged around the room, vestiges of movies gone by. A popcorn machine sat to one side of him, partially filled with the fluffy stuff. But the buttery popcorn scent wasn't the only smell in the room. Judging by the unwashed musk he recognized over-laying everything, he currently guested in the lair of one deranged mutant chimp called Lester.

And I don't think he's brought me here for a movie date night.

Perhaps it was the fact he found himself duct taped to a table unable to move anything but his head, or the various needles sticking from his body, or the mad laughter of the gibbering psycho as he pranced around singing something about what the doctor ordered, but Nolan got the impression he might be in a teensy tiny bit of trouble.

Where is my mother with her bubble ball when I need her? He could have used some over protective pride love right about now. At least the mutant didn't get his claws on Clarice. Actually, if what he gleaned from Lester's foaming speech was accurate, he'd bided his time until she left.

"I was so clever, doc—tor. So very, very clever," Lester hissed as he lumbered into sight. And what a monstrous sight. Last Nolan saw, Lester was a decent-looking guy with clean cut hair and features. Now, his face misshapen, more monster than man, his nose several times its normal size, his lips a lumpy mess and his hair sticking out in straggly clumps, Nolan could admit the guy might have a reason for his grudge. "I saw how they guarded you. Those FUCs with their guns and that annoying bird with her sharp eyes. They never left you alone. So I waited. And waited. But they kept looking. And looking. Never finding me or my old cell mates."

"You were spying on me?"

"Watching. Yes. Waiting. But I was more clever than FUC. I scared off my friends from the dungeon. Killed the ones who wouldn't go away. I knew, knew, that if I was patient, so very, very patient, that the guards would eventually leave."

"And why did you want that?" Nolan expected the answer, but figured the longer he kept Lester talking, the more time he had to find a way out—or hope for rescue. Lion strength or not, the damn monkey knew how to tape a man. Must have watched some Dexter.

"I wanted my chance to get you, of course, doc—tor."

"But why?" Nolan asked as he wiggled his fingers, testing the tightness of his bindings and hoping the chimp didn't notice the claws popping from the ends of his digits.

"Because you had to pay!" Lester raised his hands and Nolan didn't like the fact he clutched a fistful of syringes in each hand.

"Why do I have to pay? I'm not the one who hurt you. Mastermind did and she's dead."

Spittle flew as Lester replied, his crazed, bloodshot eyes rolling. "All doctors must pay! Evil creatures with your needles." Jab. "And your blood taking." Poke. "Always wanting to run more and more tests." Lester foamed at the mouth as he ranted and inserted hypodermics at random in Nolan's poor, trussed up body.

"I just wanted to help you."

"Help me? Help me! Look at me! I am a monster!" Lester screamed. "This is what helping me did? And now, you will suffer too."

The misshapen creature, more beast than man, loped around the table pushing at the needles sticking up from his skin, and Nolan winced, each pinprick a mini torture. To think people paid acupuncturists for the same kind of treatment. Then again, Nolan would take a little needlework any day over the sharp knife Lester pulled out when he tired of his pricking game.

"What are you planning to do with that, Lester?"

"You took away my life. Took away my looks. And now, I am going to return the favor." He cackled and Nolan bunched his muscles, readying himself to flex in the hopes he could break free.

"Can't we talk about this some more? Maybe over coffee? Or a box of Cracker Jacks?"

"No. I am done talking. Done listening. Done letting you ruin my life."

And Nolan was done playing nice. "Don't make me bring the lion out."

"Go ahead," Lester taunted. "I dare you to try. One of the needles I gave you had a suppressant in it. Your lion is probably sound asleep by now. Amazing what you can find on the streets these days."

Despite the chilling words, Nolan tried. He called for his feline. Ordered it to take over his body. Bellowed in his head for it to wake up, but only a hearty snore met his demands. It seemed his furry self wouldn't come to his rescue.

The psycho danced around his bound body laughing. "Told you so. Told you so. How does it feel to be a helpless patient, doc—tor? To know you're at the mercy of someone else? Time for some cosmetic surgery. Prepare to suffer." Lester grabbed a fistful of hair and yanked Nolan's head back. A moment later, Nolan bellowed.

Chapter Twenty

Forget waiting for backup, the moment Clarice heard Nolan's cry, her booted foot came up and kicked in the storage room door. The sight that met her rapier gaze took a moment to digest.

Nolan lay atop a table, trussed up tighter than a turkey at Thanksgiving. Silver tape wound around him in a cocoon while his body bristled like a porcupine as needles of varying lengths protruded from his body. Dots of blood peppered him, but it wasn't that which made her lion scream in misery. No, the reason proved more horrific than that.

As the psycho bounced away from the table, in one hand a gleaming knife, in the other a hank of hair, Nolan moaned, "No, not my mane!"

Later, she'd surely find time to snigger, probably when she wielded the scissors that would be necessary to even out her kitty's less than professional haircut, but for the moment, she needed to take down a psychotic menace who stood between her and happiness.

"Drop the knife," she ordered, her training kicking in.

Around whirled Lester, his bloodshot eyes facing in opposing directions, which sent a shudder down her spine. "Here, chicken, chicken," cooed the crazy chimp. "Come closer so I can make you into nuggets."

"Are you for real?" she asked with a snort. She took aim and before the lunatic could rush her, put a bullet in his pea-sized brain. Down went the menace. An anti-climatic moment for the merry chase he'd led them on. Sure, some people would have talked for a while, attempted an arrest, maybe engaged in hand-to-hand combat. But this was real life, not the movies, and Clarice didn't spend hours on the shooting range just to miss when the crucial time to act arrived. So, she shot to kill and ended the psycho's reign of terror.

"Clarice! You came for me!" Nolan sounded so happy and he smiled widely.

She almost blushed. "Well, someone had to."

"I'm glad it was you, but you couldn't have arrived a few minutes earlier before he maimed me?" Nolan added on a mournful note as she held up the shorn hunk of hair after rescuing it from the chimp's clenched fist.

Down to the scalp, it would take more than a comb over and a haircut to hide the damage. "Poor, Sylvester. Don't worry. It will grow back. Eventually. "

Nolan scowled, probably in reply to her smirk. "This isn't funny, Clarice. A lion's pride is his mane."

"So you'll have a Mohawk for a few weeks. Just think of your mother's face when she sees it."

"She'll hate it, won't she?"

"Most definitely."

"How did you know where to find me?" he asked as she sawed through the duct tape binding him.

"As I flew back to rescue your hairy butt," which she did in record time, despite the travel bag of clothes and weapons she wore around her neck, "I had time to mull over the few things we knew about the case. The one thing all the crime scenes Lester visited had in common was popcorn." Not only did those with a good sense of smell note the out of place odor, they'd found a few kernels and crumbs. They'd just not understood what it meant.

"The guy loved the fluffy stuff."

"It was then it hit me. Where was the one place he could get tons of it? A place currently abandoned because of an ongoing dispute with the city over a renovation permit?"

"The downtown movie theatre."

"Bingo. Acting on that assumption, I came straight here and called for backup as soon as I was sure."

"You asked for help?"

A scowl in his direction didn't wipe his incredulous look. "I did. I wasn't taking any chances with your safety."

A smug smile crossed his lips. "Because you care."

She didn't answer. Couldn't. Despite what Brenda said, Clarice wasn't ready to admit anything. Or at least not first.

With a rip, Nolan tore the partially sawed bindings holding him down and made quick work of those around his legs. As he freed himself from the table, Clarice watched, unsure of what to say. Unsure of what he'd do. What would happen next? What—

Forget finding out anytime soon. A wave of FUC agents, with their guns drawn, poured into the tight space, shouting out orders. Nolan wasn't the only one whipping his hands up screaming don't shoot. Thankfully, no one got trigger happy, and despite the obvious, began asking questions. People jostled in front of her, tending to her lion, and feeling in the way, Clarice slipped out the door, unsure of what she should do or where she should go.

A roar made her look back, but she couldn't see Nolan with all the agents in the way.

"Clarice!" Nolan bellowed again. "Don't you dare fly off on me again, woman. We need to talk."

Leaning against the wall, she didn't reply, just waited, and sure enough, a tousled-haired man with wild eyes came bounding out, wearing only boxers, with needles still sticking out at random. She winced at the reminder of his torture. "You should let a doctor take care of that."

Peering down, Nolan growled as he tore the syringes out. "I am a doctor. And I'm fine. Or will be as soon as you and I clear something up. Why did you leave me?"

"It was getting crowded in there."

"Not now. Before."

She lifted a shoulder. "My office ordered me back."

"So you just left without saying goodbye?"

"It seemed like the best thing at the time."

"Best thing? All the time we spent together, the things we shared, the things we felt, and you left without even talking to me."

"I left a note."

Nolan crossed his arms, but didn't look impressed.

Noticing the curious eyes peeking through the door, she shifted uncomfortably. "Must we discuss this here?"

"Yes, we must. See, I'm not taking the chance you'll just fly off again. Not before I've said my piece." He took a deep breath and she braced herself for another harangue. "I love you, Clarice."

She gaped at him. *Did he just say what I think he said?* "What?"

"I said. I. Love. You. As in, I-want-you-to-spend-the-rest-of-your-life-with-me love you."

Her heart thumped madly. "But you're a cat. I'm a bird."

"So?"

"So, your mother will never stand for it."

"Don't care. I love you. I want you to come back to me."

"Even if your family hates me?"

"They don't hate you."

"Then why does your cousin Yanna keep emailing me stuffing recipes?"

He grinned. "Because you keep sending her the different Cat Chow commercials with that stupid jingle."

Clarice's lips curled in amusement at the reminder. "I won't promise to sit at home like a good girl. I'll probably want to work for FUC as an agent."

"I'm good with that."

"I won't pick up your dirty socks."

"What a coincidence. Neither will I."

She glared at him. "If we're going to be together, then you can't expect the women of your pride to keep taking care of you."

"Fine. I'll clean up after myself if you learn how to cook.

"On second thought, those felines are nothing but mischief when they've got too much time on their paws. Maybe we'll let them keep doing some stuff. But I won't have your mother meddling and sticking her whiskers in my business."

"Good luck with that. I've been trying for years."

"I also might still succumb to the urge to tell bad Garfield jokes and buy her cat toys."

"And I look forward to the entertainment of you driving her wild."

"I won't change."

"No one's asking you to. The only thing I want from you is your love. Can you love me, Clarice?"

Looking at her toes, all too aware of the audience watching and listening, Clarice really wanted to flee, flap her wings and leave, fear of giving her heart still so strong. A finger tilted her chin up and Nolan's steady gaze caught hers. "I won't ever leave you, Clarice. Nor do I want you to be anything less than who you are. Trust in me."

Tears threatening, and her throat stupidly tight, she whispered the words she'd never said aloud for anyone. "I love you."

She barely heard the cheer that erupted as his lips swooped in to claim hers in a searing kiss. She clung to her lion—*yes, my lion*—and wondered how she could have ever walked away in the first place. How could she not have seen the signs of his love?

She could have kissed him forever, but the back thumping and congratulations got to be intrusive and they separated, reluctantly. Even though they couldn't continue to kiss, or leave quite yet, Nolan refused to leave her side. His fingers remained meshed with hers at all times as they answered questions, and she fought not to blush whenever he shot an intimate smile her way.

At one point, she lost her grip on him as his mother bullied her way past the agents and drew him into a bone-crushing hug. Clarice rolled her eyes as Brenda ranted and raved over the damage done to her poor baby boy.

When it got to the point she felt her lunch might come up, she interrupted. "Sylvester, I realize you're bonding with Mommy, but do you want to cut the apron strings so we can go home, or would you prefer to suck the teat a while longer and keep me waiting?"

Nolan choked. Mason doubled over. Jaws dropped everywhere and several bystanders took a few steps back, clearing the area.

Clarice smirked at Brenda, waiting for the explosion.

"Have I mentioned how much I love this girl?" His mother beamed. At her. "You are going to make my son a wonderful wife. We'll plan for a spring wedding."

Excuse me? What just happened? "What did you say?"

"Well, you can't expect my boy to live in sin. We'll announce it by the weekend, as soon as I can get the announcement to the *Shifter Times*."

"You will do nothing of the sort," Clarice growled.

Brenda went on as if she'd not said a word. "I'm thinking of a pastel-colored theme. Lots of pink. What do you think, *daughter?*"

"No one said anything about a wedding." Clarice must have shown signs of flight, because Nolan's hand gripped her tight, grounding her.

Brenda smiled an evil, catty grin. "Now, now, Tweety. Don't you worry your pretty little bird brain about a thing. Mother will take care of everything."

Oh yeah, that harsh panting was her hyperventilating. "Didn't you hear me? I said no. Nolan, do something. I am not getting married. Why can't we just nest together? I'm okay with shacking up"

"I know, but love me, have to put up with my mother. Congratulations. Welcome to my world. You're now part of the pride. You'll be glad to know they serve homemade cookies."

"She can't do this."

Nolan patted her hand. "Just go with the flow. It's easier. And hey, if she's planning a wedding then at least she won't be hassling us to make a baby."

She blanched. "Oh pigeon poop. I'd not even thought of that."

"Babies? Did someone say babies?"

Before Clarice could fend off the overwhelming attention of a mother-in-law bent on making her into the daughter she never had, they fled, commandeering a FUC vehicle, which wasn't as nice as his Audi, and smaller. Not that Nolan seemed to care. He still managed to curl on his side and lay his head in her lap. He also closed his eyes.

"Do not tell me you're going to nap now."

He opened one lazy orb. "You're here. We're safe. I'm horny. And once we get to my place, I don't intend to let you sleep until we've both come at least a half dozen times."

With that kind of logic, she hummed him a lullaby as she stroked his massacred mane. She also broke a few speed limits getting them back to his condo where he put his nap to good use until she promised to never leave him ever again. And to love him forever.

Scary or not, she'd not only fallen in love with a lion, she now had a family. Damned dust in the air.

Epilogue

When Brenda's wedding frenzy got to be too much—the last straw being the eighteen-tiered cake topped with a giant lion wearing a falcon on his back—Nolan enacted his secret plan, which Clarice thanked him for in a most orally satisfying fashion.

They eloped and ended up on a beach in Hawaii. Minutes before sunset, they got married, just the priest, him, Clarice, the surf, sand, and three hundred of his mother's closest friends. How she managed to get them all out there on such short notice and without Clarice spotting them, Nolan never figured out, but in the end, he got what he wanted.

A wife. And Clarice got what she needed, love—in the form of a dysfunctional feline family who took to their new avian family member with gusto. What his poor falcon didn't expect when she fell in love with a lion, though, was the advice.

"A male lion needs a firm whack on the nose every day to keep him in line."

"No, you ninny. Just keep him fed and he'll be the best pussycat around."

"Lazy feline bastards. You should have never married him. It's much more fun to live in sin."

"I can't believe you don't intend to share."

His poor Clarice, she appeared quite overwhelmed.

"How do you stand it?" she moaned when they finally escaped their well-meaning—and occasional poultry-stuffing—advice.

"For the most part, I ignore them."

"I tried that. I don't think they noticed because they kept on talking."

"Count yourself lucky. It means they like you."

"Couldn't they like me a little less?"

"Doubtful. It's your own fault for being so darned lovable."

And she was. On the outside and to others, she might present a rude and sometimes crude façade, but when it was just the two of them, the real Clarice let her hair down and showed him over and over again why he fell in love with her.

Under the stars and the moon shining through their honeymoon cottage skylight, they indulged in their passion as man and wife. At the height of her orgasm, she roared in pleasure. He then, of course, roared louder, just to prove a point. Then she made him purr, proving her own point. A lion and a falcon, together forever—

"So now that the wedding is over, when are you getting started on making babies?" His mother's interruption couldn't have happened at a worse moment.

Nolan napped as his new wife chased his mother down the beach, her falcon form swooping and diving at the bounding lioness. But as he dozed, he smiled. Married life with his falcon would definitely never be boring.

*

Meanwhile, miles away from FUC headquarters…

Out she ventured from the edge of the woods with dainty steps that still crushed the foliage underfoot. Bleary-eyed, he tried to make sense of what he saw, but couldn't, his injuries too great, his mind not working at full speed.

He tried to speak, or at least let her know who he worked for. He croaked a feeble, "FUC."

The timid creature recoiled and bounded back into the forest.

A groan left him as he realized he'd just tried to speak with a plain old woodland creature. It seemed his sense of smell was shot, right along with his poor body. That didn't bode well.

Half in, half out of the water, he managed to roll to his stomach and claw his way further up the muddy embankment, a few feet of torture that left him panting.

Black spots danced before his eyes. He could feel the dark nirvana hovering over him, waiting to grab him in its embrace. He needed to fight it. Needed to…

The next time he woke, which surprised him greatly, he did so under a wooden slatted roof, on a bed covered in a blanket smelling oddly enough of lilacs. He knew the scent because his mother liked to grow them when he was boy on the farm. He could still hear his father grumble about the darned things taking up valuable farmland space, but despite that, he allowed them just because they made his mother smile.

Do the lilacs mean I'm home? No. Because home had white plaster ceilings and the mincing steps approaching did not belong to his mother. Not to mention, his mother never tied him to a bed. *Uh-oh.*

The end…for now.

More Books by Eve Langlais

Published by Amira Press:
Alien Mate, Alien Mate 2, Alien Mate 3
Broomstick Breakdown
Dating Cupid
Mated To The Devil
Pack Series: Defying Pack Law, Betraying The Pack, Seeking Pack Redemption
Taming Her Wolf
His Teddy Bear
Scared of Spiders
The Hunter (Realm series)

Published by Liquid Silver Books:
Princess of Hell series: Lucifer's Daughter, Snowballs In Hell, Hell's Revenge
Hybrid Misfit
Last Minion Standing
Toxic

Published by Eve Langlais
The Geek Job
Furry United Coalition: Bunny And The Bear, Swan And The Bear, Croc And The Fox, Lion and the Falcon
Freakn' Shifters: Delicate Freakn' Flower, Jealous And Freakn', Already Freakn' Mated, Jungle Freakn' Bride
Alien Abduction: Accidental Abduction, Intentional Abduction, Dual Abduction, Mercenary Abduction
Cyborgs: More Than Machines: C791, F814, B785
Welcome To Hell: A Demon And His Witch, A Demon And His Psycho

Author Biography

Hello and thanks for taking the time to read something I wrote. I do hope I managed to entertain you – and make you giggle a time or two. Since you're actually checking out this note, I guess it means you're curious about me, so here's the scoop.

I am a mom of three, who is just shy of forty. I am married (over thirteen years now) to a man whom I adore – when he's not driving me insane. A true romantic, I totally believe in love at first sight. But then again, I also think there is life 'out' there – hopefully as sexy as the aliens I've created in my mind. Lol.

I am Canadian, but being a military brat, I've been coast to coast. Right now, I'm living in the Ottawa area – hockey, poutine and beavertails, yay – and enjoying the chaos of family life.

If you want to know more about me, then I guess I should mention you can visit me at

http://www.EveLanglais.com

Sexy covers, excerpts, my blog, and other items that might interest you, await.

Until we meet in the pages of a book again, wishing you tons of great reading and smiles,

Eve

Made in the USA
Lexington, KY
11 September 2013